jill mars the United Kingdom to New Zealand, along with her small daughter and her even smaller mad dog. Her childhood ambition was to become an author, so in 2001 Jill gave up her career at a huge international company to concentrate on writing for children. When not working, writing and being a mum, Jill plays guitar, takes singing lessons and is learning to play the drum kit she has set up in the garage. One day she might even sing in a band again . . .

Look out for the fifth book in the
jane blonde series:

jane blonde, goldenspy

Jane Blonde

spylet on ice

JILL MARSHALL

MACMILLAN CHILDREN'S BOOKS

First published 2007 by Macmillan Children's Books
a division of Macmillan Publishers Limited
20 New Wharf Road, London N1 9RR
Basingstoke and Oxford
www.panmacmillan.com

Associated companies throughout the world

ISBN: 978-0-330-44658-7

1 3 5 7 9 8 6 4 2

A CIP catalogue record for this book is available from
the British Library.

Typeset by Nigel Hazle
Printed and bound in Great Britain by Mackays of Chatham plc, Kent

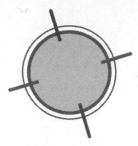

thanks to glenys, rachel and talya, who often know better than i do what i'm thinking, and to angie for getting me out and about in nz. special thanks to mum and dad for cooking, cleaning, child-minding, gardening and general diy (did i miss anything?) during the writing of this book. we should do it more often! and with apologies for being confusing last time, thanks to emma bower and molly codyre for being jb fans, and having smiley faces at the crossing every morning . . .

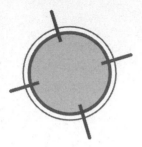

for kelly and jayne, for being there
(both mentally and in the jimmy t)
from the very beginning.
miss you guys!

contents

1	scan the plan	1
2	icy invitations	10
3	spicamp spirit	19
4	satispies and spyroscopes	37
5	tumble-tubes	48
6	titian ambition	60
7	snowdome	71
8	blonde to the rescue	81
9	icebergs, spicebergs	90
10	sol's lols revisited	100
11	out in the cold	110
12	woe for worms	119
13	poles and penguins	129
14	zinc or zwim	142
15	prawn cocktail	155
16	sons and saviours	166

17	clarification	175
18	alfie and ralfie	186
19	melting monsters	199
20	sick squid	212
21	tunnel of terror	223
22	spud nik in space	236
23	abe's babes	245

scan the plan

Janey Brown awoke the instant she heard the parcel thump on to the floor. She flicked her mousey hair from her eyes and leaped out of bed. Thumping parcels usually meant one thing, and one thing only – a message from her father. Of course there was the odd disappointment when the package actually turned out to be something from one of her mum's catalogues, but Janey now had enough of an instinct for this kind of thing to guess when something was afoot. This was one of those moments, she was sure.

It was only a few months since plain Janey Brown had discovered that she was actually Jane Blonde, Sensational Spylet, but in that time she had truly grown into the role. Her gadgets ('SPI-buys', to Blonde and her spy friends) usually got her out of trouble – apart from when they flung her straight into it. Spy friends from her father's organization, SPI – Solomon's Polifications Investigations – had formed a tight-knit group

1

around her: there was G-Mamma, her vibrant and rather *unusual* mentor; the Halos, headteacher Mrs Halliday and her son (and Janey's best friend) Alfie; Trouble the Spycat; Maddy the spy sheep; and recently Bert, Australian ex-sheep farmer turned spy recruit.

And the very, very best revelation of all: that her father was not dead as she had believed for all her pre-spying days, but was super-SPI Boz 'Brilliance' Brown, head of SPI and able to change his identity by means of his own miraculous scientific discoveries. Janey never knew whether he would be Boz or his alter ego Solomon Brown or businessman extraordinaire Abe Rownigan. What Janey did know, however, was that whenever her dad sent her a parcel, it was bound to have a secret, spy purpose.

She raced down the stairs in her pyjamas, focusing on the doormat. Sure enough, there was a flattish cardboard box, just about the right size to have squeezed through the letter box. It was addressed to Janey Brown, in a logoed envelope from the Sol's Lols ice-lolly factory in Scotland. Sol's Lols was another of the businesses her father operated to disguise his spying activities, along with Abe 'n' Jean's Clean Machines, which he ran with her mother. The smiley round face of Sol the lolly-maker beamed at her above the words: 'Be sure to shop for Sol's Lols!'

Janey's mum appeared from the kitchen, holding a cup of tea. 'I thought that would probably be for you – seeing as you're the only one who ever gets any interesting parcels.'

Jean Brown raised an eyebrow at her daughter, and Janey suddenly saw in her the super-SPI that she used to be. Recently Gina Bellarina had returned to her former glory for a few brief moments and fought alongside the husband she had believed to be dead. But any memory of that, and of all other spy-related events, had been completely wiped from Gina's brain, and she had gone back to being Jean Brown of the Clean Jean Cleaning Company and of Abe 'n' Jean's Clean Machines.

'It's from . . . Uncle Sol, I think,' said Janey, parting the gum around the edges carefully. She never knew whether the message would be contained within the package, or would be part of the envelope itself. A solid glass photo frame slid out on to her bare toe. 'Ow! That's cold! I hope I haven't broken it.'

She picked up the frame anxiously. 'Oh, it's a penguin,' she said in surprise.

Jean Brown peered over her shoulder. 'He always sends you such odd gifts. Why on earth would you want a picture of a penguin? Maybe we could take it out and use the frame for something useful.'

She reached out to take the photograph from her daughter, but Janey clutched it to her chest. 'No! No, I really like penguins. We've been, um, studying them at school, so this is great.'

Her mother cocked her head quizzically, just as someone knocked at the door. Glad of the distraction, Janey flung it open to find her friend and fellow

Spylet, Alfie Halliday, clutching a very familiar-looking brown package.

'Snap,' he said, shaking the envelope so that an identical glass frame slid out on to his outstretched hand. Suddenly he noticed Mrs Brown standing behind Janey and blushed to the roots of his chestnut hair. How would they explain their way out of this one? 'Err, morning, Mrs B. Off to work soon?'

'It's Saturday,' said Jean Brown. 'Even cleaners get a day off, you know. Now, isn't that strange? Janey's received exactly the same parcel from her uncle. Do you know Solomon Brown too?'

'I . . . no. No, I don't. But I . . . buy a lot of lollies. Love them. Favourite thing,' muttered Alfie.

Janey jumped in to help him out. 'I expect they've got your name on a database somewhere from . . . from . . .'

'. . . that competition I did.' Alfie nodded enthusiastically. 'S'right. Win a year's worth of ice lollies.'

'So Uncle Sol must have sent this picture to lots of people,' said Janey. 'Not just me.'

Jean Brown looked from one to the other of them, eyes narrowed over her tea cup as they both smiled brightly at her. 'Well, it sounds like something he would do,' she said eventually. 'Marketing, I suppose. It's all about sales, isn't it? It even says so on the envelope. I'm sorry, Janey.' She put an arm around Janey's shoulders. 'I though this time he might have sent you something special, just for you. Not just some freebie to make you buy his products.'

But Janey knew that she had been sent something extremely special. 'I don't mind,' she said, popping the package into her bag that was propped against the banister. 'He's probably got some special offer on or something. Alfie, maybe we should go to the supermarket and find out?'

Alfie shrugged, looking a little annoyed that Janey seemed to have worked something out before him. This was often the case. 'I've got an hour before football,' he said grudgingly.

'Great!' Janey went to step out of the door, but as she did so her mum grabbed her arm.

'Two things, darling. One, you're still in your pyjamas. And two, if you're going shopping, you could get a few bits and pieces for me.' She fished in her purse. 'Some Brie, crackers and grapes, and some tortilla chips and dip. I think that should do it.'

'OK,' said Janey, bewildered. It didn't sound like their usual Saturday tea, but maybe her mum had got so sick of cooking (as she did it so badly) that she'd decided on cold food only in future.

'Fifty-six minutes until football.' Alfie pointed at his watch, and within moments Janey was back downstairs in jeans, T-shirt and cardigan.

They cycled to the supermarket on Alfie's SPI-cycle, Janey sitting on the seat clutching both packages,

5

and Alfie standing on the pedals to propel them along. They went on a strange, convoluted route through alleys and backstreets to avoid being seen by any non-spies. The SPI-cycle stayed proudly upright as Alfie spun them around corners, along pavements, and over the odd fence – straight up one side and just as straight down the other. Reaching Pick-and-Save in only moments, they headed for the aisle containing Frozen Confectionery.

'Wall's, own-brand, Viennettas . . . where is the Sol's Lols stuff?' said Alfie, striding impatiently along the row. 'Why can't he just pick up the phone and give us a message the normal way?'

'Because then we wouldn't be Spylets,' said Janey, with that special thrill that went through her whenever she remembered she was not just Janey Brown, schoolgirl and dutiful daughter, but also Jane Blonde, ace spy-in-training. 'Here they are. Look for one with a penguin on it.'

Resting the packages on top of the other ice creams, Janey and Alfie leaned over the freezer and sifted through the Sol's Lols products. Within moments their breath felt as though it were sticking to their cheeks, and their hands were aching with cold.

'Wish I had my Boy-battler on,' said Alfie, referring to the super-charged glove he wore when he went through the Wower and turned into Spylet Al Halo. The spy shower transformed anyone within it, adding gadgets and gizmos and, occasionally, mission-appropriate clothing.

Janey wished for her Girl-gauntlet too. 'My fingers are dropping off,' moaned Alfie. 'Look, do you seriously think he's planted a message in an ice lolly in the local Pick-and-Save? Anyone could pick it up and walk off with it.'

Janey paused, rubbing her hands together. 'That's a good point. Some toddler could be eating the information right now. He wouldn't risk it. So what else could it be?'

A cross-faced supermarket worker was bearing down on them. 'What are you doing in there? It'll take me ages to put them all back in the right boxes! Just choose one and clear off.'

'Actually, we don't want one now,' said Janey. 'Sorry.'

Both Spylets made some half-hearted attempts to smooth over the stirred-up lolly section, then picked up their packages and ran. Janey skidded to a halt next to the cheese. 'I'd better get this stuff for my mum first, and then we'll try something else.'

'I don't have time,' said Alfie. 'Football's in quarter of an hour.'

'Well, what's more important?' said Janey impatiently, but she knew what the answer would be. While they were on a mission, Alfie was a million per cent dedicated. Right now, however, when they weren't getting very far, she guessed that the footy pitch was looking very attractive. 'Oh, OK. I'll walk home.'

Janey wandered listlessly round the supermarket,

picking up the items on her shopping list. The morning wasn't turning out to be quite as exciting or satisfactory as she'd imagined. Furthermore, the package from Uncle Sol had become freezing cold from being placed on top of the lollies, so cold it was actually burning her skin through her T-shirt. She stopped and tipped it into the basket of cheese and crackers.

As the frame slid out of the packaging slightly, she looked again at the penguin. Maybe she should be looking elsewhere. Penguin biscuits? Or fish that penguins might eat? It was a bit of a puzzle, and she was normally so good at those. But then she looked more closely at the space above the penguin's head. Etched into the glass was a little series of upright lines, like a broken fence, with a row of tiny numbers underneath. She'd seen one before, she was sure of it. Something to do with maths at school? No. Closer to home. A series of bars. A run of numbers that could be a code. Now she'd thought it through, it was completely obvious. 'Those things they put on tins for scanning. A bar code!' said Janey. How had she failed to notice it before?

She had everything she needed, so Janey raced to the checkout and waited anxiously in the queue, hopping from one foot to the other. At last it was her turn, and she turned the basket upside down on to the conveyor belt, holding the penguin photo under her cardigan so it couldn't be seen.

'That's fifteen seventy-five,' said the till operator.

Perfect. Dipping into her pocket, Janey pulled out a couple of notes and a handful of coins and flung them towards the lady behind the till. As she'd hoped, a couple of the coins catapulted across the other side of the conveyor belt and disappeared down the side of the till operator's seat. Tutting loudly, the woman clambered down off the chair and scrabbled on the ground for the money.

She only had a split second. Opening up her cardigan, Janey swept her arm in front of the scanner. Nothing. She did it again, wondering what the man behind her in the queue would think of her flapping her purple-clad arm around like a bat-wing. Still nothing. The woman was straightening up, turning around, and Janey had no time to lose. Grabbing the edge of the photo frame with her left hand, she located the bar code and aimed it straight at the front of the scanner. There was a faint beep, and Janey caught her breath as she spotted writing and images filling the small glass panel in the centre of the photo frame.

'School project,' she said to the man behind her, then shoved the frame firmly beneath her cardigan as she picked up her bag of shopping. Wishing she was wearing her Fleet-feet, she sprinted for home, or rather for the home next door to her own. G-Mamma's Spylab was what she needed now.

icy invitations

'Have you ever even heard of SPIcamp?' said Janey excitedly.

G-Mamma shook her head as Janey stared, fascinated, at the images from the glass photo frame now projected on to the front of G-Mamma's enormous white fridge. Several spies-in-training were Fleet-footing around an assault course, using all sorts of SPI-buys to fight off the other team and be first to the finish line. There were Girl-gauntlets and Boy-battlers, SuSPInders (a retractable long rope with a strong winch), SPIders, which looked like bubblegum but were actually SPI Direct Energy Replenishment devices, able to supply oxygen under water, and a couple Janey had never seen before. It looked fun – like Laserquest, only with real spy weapons. Above the image sat a couple of lines of flamboyant fuchsia writing:

Congratulations on decoding your personal invitation to SPIcamp.
Your SPI:KE will receive a LipSPICK with details.
See you soon!

'Did you do this when you were a Spylet?' Janey asked her own SPI:KE – her SPI Kid Educator.

'No way, Blonday.' G-Mamma shrugged. 'SPIcamp is a new thing. Your dad must have just introduced it – maybe as a way to get closer to you.'

Janey smiled as a small glow ignited within her and she looked again at the moving images. She had now met up with her father on several missions; it wouldn't altogether surprise her if what G-Mamma said was true. And she loved being able to support him – to step into the Wower, transform herself from ordinary schoolgirl Janey Brown and help her father fight off evil baddies.

Abe Rownigan's voice, filtering through the speakers disguised as a bread-maker and a microwave on either side of the fridge, was now pointing out the various features of the SPIcamp. 'Once you've mastered all the units, you'll be a fully fledged member of the SPI Academy, which entitles you to call yourself a spy. I think you'll find it a lot of fun, and very inspiring. I've hand-selected the coordinators and all the students and their SPI:KEs, and you should all bring along your spy-pet, if you have one.'

'All?' said Janey. 'How many of us do you think there'll be?'

G-Mamma didn't seem to be anywhere near as excited as Janey. 'He IS kidding, right? SPI:KE?! Me? Retraining? I don't need a refresher, unless it's the sweetie kind that comes in a packet.'

'G-Mamma, it'll be fun! We'll get to meet some other spies and Spylets, get the latest SPI-buys, try out some new technology . . .'

'Oh yes, and what else?' G-Mamma put her gold fingernail against her pouting glossy lips. 'I know! See your father again!' she said pointedly. She knew exactly why Janey was so keen to go.

'Do you think he'll be there?' said Janey, a little breathless with bottled-up hope.

'Your father,' said G-Mamma, popping a meat-and-potato pie into the microwave, 'is a mystery to all of us. Only he knows where he'll spring up next, and whose body he'll be occupying to do it. And that is a very good thing,' she added sternly.

Janey avoided her gaze. There had been occasions when she had been a bit too quick to believe that someone might or might not be her dad – not realizing that Abe Rownigan was actually 'A Brown Again' and genuinely her father, for instance, but accepting without question a slightly odd version of Abe who had turned out to be Copernicus, arch-enemy and evil overlord, posing as her father in a fake copy of his body. G-Mamma was taking

a little while to forgive her for it completely. 'I'll . . . um
. . . just go and call Alfie – tell him about the barcode and
what have you.'

The pie blocking G-Mamma's face nodded up and
down so Janey hopped off the tall stool at the Spylab
computer bench, whistled for Trouble the Spycat, and
glided on her ASPIC (Aeronautical SPI Conveyor)
through the tunnel that linked the fireplace in the Spylab
with Janey's own, ordinary bedroom in the house next
door.

'Alfie,' she cried as he picked up the phone, 'check
your penguin photo! There's a bar code on it.'

'Well, I would, but the frame sort of seems to have
melted.'

'What?'

Alfie sighed. 'Melted. Just the little photo of the
penguin left, a bit soggy now.'

'But mine hasn't melted. Why would yours?'

'Dunno. Although it might be because . . .' He
sounded a little sheepish. 'I'm on kit-washing duty this
week. I put it in the bag with all the strips after the
match.'

Janey thought about the sweaty clothing and decided
not to ask any more. 'So that must mean they're made
of ice, not glass. That would explain why it felt cold,
and why the code appeared after we'd put them in the
freezer.'

'Well, duh, obviously . . .' It wasn't obvious

13

at all, but Alfie wasn't going to let Janey get away with solving all the clues herself. 'And why it's melted. They're formed to self-destruct after a certain amount of time, and he's used steganography. Clever,' he said approvingly.

'What's stega-wotsit?'

Janey could almost hear Alfie preening. 'It's the art of hiding messages. The Greeks did it by shaving some dude's head, tattooing it and waiting for his hair to grow back. Then the person at the other end got the message by shaving his head again. Don't tell me you didn't know that?'

At this, Janey heard a scuffle on the other end, and suddenly found she was hearing Alfie's mother, Mrs Halliday. 'Janey, I've just this minute told him about steganography. Don't let him get all superior, especially when he's forgetting to ask you the most important part: what did the message say?'

'It's an invitation to SPIcamp.'

'And your mum will let you go?'

'Oh no!'

It was a very good point. There was no way Clean Jean would believe tales of a spycamp, and even less hope that she would let Janey attend.

'Don't worry,' said Mrs Halliday. 'I'll call your mum and say we're going off on some hothousing week for gifted children or something.'

Janey grinned. Her mum loved her to pieces but

probably wouldn't believe for an instant that she was gifted, unless, of course, somebody influential told her it was true – someone like Alfie's mum, super-SPI Maisie Halo and headmistress of Janey's school. 'Brilliant.'

It *would* be brilliant, she knew it. Janey's spy instincts were all ablaze, and she really couldn't wait to be at SPIcamp, learning new things, meeting new spies, and – hopefully – getting to know her dad better than ever. It was a chance she just couldn't miss. Alfie had wrestled the phone back off his mother. 'We'll pick you up in the morning. SPIcamp – yesss!' The phone went dead.

Janey wandered into the lounge. Her mum was sitting like an island in an ocean of documents, working her way methodically through the accounts for the little chain of companies she now managed. 'Sweetheart,' she said distractedly, 'make me a cup of tea, will you? My brain isn't working properly. This final sum is wrong, I'm sure.'

Janey looked at her sensible mum, doing sensible things with a calculator, and wondered how she could have truly forgotten what it was like to be a spy. 'Not enough money?'

'No,' said Jean, shaking the calculator as if that would make it come up with a different figure. 'No, quite the opposite. Too much. I mean, if this thing is right, we've made more money than I could ever have imagined. I think we might actually be . . . well, quite wealthy.'

'Mum, that's great!' said Janey, giving her a hug. 'You've worked so hard. And that means we can have loads and loads of pizza!' It was their special Friday-night treat – pizza and a DVD, slippers on and the week shrugged off like an old coat.

Jean smiled, a little bewildered. 'I suppose so. And I suppose . . . well, if the accountant says this is all correct, we can do all sorts. Move to a bigger house! Imagine, Janey, I could have a proper office at home, and you could have friends over to stay!'

Janey thought quickly. If they moved house, G-Mamma would also have to move so that the Spylab remained close by. 'But I love this house. Anyway, this address is on all your business stuff.' As proof she held up a piece of paper bearing the Abe 'n' Jean emblem.

'True,' said Jean. 'Well, even if we don't move house, let's have a proper holiday this summer! I'll call the travel agents and see what they suggest. We could go anywhere!'

Her mum looked so thrilled and excited that Janey's heart sank as the phone rang. Little did Jean suspect that she was about to find out that not only were they reasonably well off now, but she'd also rather suddenly acquired a gifted child, who would be off to a special camp tomorrow morning. Without her.

Janey sighed and went into the kitchen. It was definitely time for that cup of tea.

Her mum walked in behind her, looking a little glum.

16

'You'll never guess who that was, Janey. Mrs Halliday says you're invited to a special hothousing week for gifted children. She thinks you'll do very well and might even get that scholarship to Everdene. I had no idea . . .'

' . . . that I was gifted? I'm not really. I think it's just that I'm good at maths.'

Her mother shook her head vigorously. 'No, I've always known you were special, Janey. I just meant I had no idea you were growing up so fast. Off for a whole week on your own. I'm so proud of you, darling.'

Janey didn't think this would be a very good time to tell her mum that she'd been away for as long before; it was simply that Jean had been in the company of a Janey-clone and hadn't realized her real daughter was away on a mission.

Janey remembered that she was supposed to be surprised. 'Wow! A week away? I'll call you lots and lots. And I'll be back before you know it.'

She smiled at her mum, but was suddenly rather taken aback. The expression on her mum's face was very peculiar – sort of . . . furtive. And a little smiley, as if she was biting back some great secret.

'Actually, darling,' Jean said in a sudden rush, 'I may be quite busy anyway. You see, I know you're going to be doing your own thing more and more, so I've decided it's time I got out and about a bit more too. I'm going to start, well, dating, I suppose you might call it.'

Janey's bottom jaw nearly hit the floor. Jean

couldn't! It wasn't right! Her mum was . . . well, old. Too old for dating. And not only was Janey used to having her mum to herself, but she also knew what her mum didn't – that Jean Brown's husband was alive and well, and desperate for them all to be together as a family again.

'Well,' she managed to say in a strangled tone after a few moments' awkward silence, 'you can wait until I'm back for that, can't you?'

Her mum looked at her sideways again. 'Um. Well, Joy from the office is quite keen to join me. She's coming for lunch tomorrow to, you know, plan our attack. We thought we'd try speed-dating.'

Janey gaped again. So that was what the posh cheese and nibbles were for! She felt as though she'd just paid for her own funeral. And what on earth was speed-dating? Jean had seemed happy enough on her own for so long, but now she wanted to find someone in double-quick time! It was even more critical that her dad was at this SPIcamp. She didn't just have him to save from whatever evils befell him, it seemed that now she had to save her mum too.

And for the first time she realized that, while being a spy could be pretty testing, being a daughter could be tough too. Grabbing a handful of the grapes she had so carefully selected, Janey stomped out of the kitchen and headed for the Spylab. At least in there she knew where she stood.

spicamp spirit

By the time the alarm went off the next morning, Janey had been ready for two and a half hours. Her little suitcase was standing to attention beside her bed, packed with jeans, T-shirts and hooded sweatshirts, underwear and toiletries. G-Mamma had been left in charge of packing Janey's SPIsuit and SPI-buys separately, in case Jean insisted on looking through her daughter's case. Janey hoped her SPI:KE had done better than the last time she'd packed for her, when all she'd put in were Trouble, some babyish pyjamas and a bunch of Day-Glo jewellery.

Janey hadn't heard her mum get up, so she crept across to her bedroom and pushed open the door. The room was empty, and the bed didn't even look slept in. 'Mum?'

'Morning, darling.' Her mum, looking pale and tired, peeked out from behind a tower of towels on the stairs behind Janey.

'You must have been up a long time,' said Janey suspiciously. She looked pretty much the same way herself when she'd been out on an all-night spying mission.

'I didn't go to bed,' said Jean, smothering a yawn. 'By the time I finished off all that accounting and stopped wondering what I was going to do without you for a whole week, it was dawn.'

'You'd better get some sleep before your ... special dating lunch.' The words came out all hard and brittle, as if her mum was going out torturing puppies instead of having Brie and walnut crackers with a friend from work.

'Oh, Janey, I will, but ...' said Jean, nodding briskly to hide the tears in her eyes. 'Oh, they're here. Got everything? Come on then, let's go.'

Janey clambered in next to Alfie in the large eight-seater people carrier. 'Not blubbing are you, Brown?' said Alfie.

'No, but I think Mum might be,' she whispered back. 'Can we get it over with?'

'Off we go then!' called Mrs Halliday cheerily, shoving the car into gear. 'Don't worry about a thing, Jean. I'll have her back to you in one piece in a week, and Janey will call every day.'

'Of course,' said Jean, waving a little forlornly. 'Enjoy yourself, Janey. You too, Alfie.'

'Bye, Mum!'

Now that she was actually going, Janey was horribly sorry at leaving her mum that way. She waved furiously until they turned the corner and drove out of sight. Moments later they were screeching to a halt at a temporary bus stop, where a chubby hand in fingerless gloves and a collection of glittering rings was flagging them down. G-Mamma looked as if she was wearing a duvet, so padded and layered was she. On closer inspection, Janey realized that she was wearing all her clothes at once, and Trouble the cat was wrapped around her neck like a fox-fur, just as he had been when Janey had first seen him.

Mrs Halliday sighed as she pulled over. 'I thought you were travelling light?'

'This is light!' G-Mamma hauled herself into the very back seat, manoeuvring herself with difficulty past Janey and Alfie and shoving two small silver suitcases over towards the boot. 'Look at the size of my bag – it's teeny. And the other one's got Janey's spygear in it, so don't blame me for that one.' She sprawled across the seat, panting.

Alfie had to reach over to do up her seat belt. 'We're going to need a crane to get her out again,' he muttered.

'I heard that, Alfie Ralfie. I'm also wearing a SPI-Pod, you might like to know.' She pointed her chins at the SPI listening/tracking device strapped to her arm.

Janey changed the subject to keep the peace.

'So where is this SPIcamp? Shouldn't we Satispy our way over?'

'And get turned into SPI-group soup? I don't think so, Zany Janey,' said G-Mamma. She had a point – the SPI satellite transporter did have a nasty habit of mixing up people's cells as it beamed them off via a dish in space to reassemble them somewhere else. 'It's not far, anyway. We'll just head up the motorway a bit and we'll be there in no time. Watch out for the weather front.'

'What's a weather front?' asked Janey.

'It's a front made of weather,' said Alfie. 'Duh.'

Mrs Halliday tutted. 'Well, sort of. It's a boundary between two air masses with different characteristics.'

'Easier my way.' Alfie stared out of the window, but there was no weather front to be seen, so he settled down with his games console as Janey pressed her nose against the glass.

Before too long they turned off the motorway and made their way through a string of little villages. It was a glorious early-summer day, and the shops selling ice creams were already busy. Only the fact that she couldn't get out of the car very easily prevented G-Mamma from leaping out to grab a Magnum or two. The hum of the engine and the whirr of the air conditioning were just lulling Janey off to sleep when suddenly she noticed something.

'It's raining,' she said, pointing to a droplet of water on the glass.

'So it is.' Mrs Halliday looked through the windscreen up at the skies, then turned her head left and right, scanning the fields around them. 'There's the weather front,' she said, 'behind that paddock with the horses. Hold on, everyone.'

With that, she yanked the steering wheel hard left and took off across the fields, much to the puzzlement of the farmer who had been about to drive his tractor out on to the road. G-Mamma peered at him through the back windscreen. 'It's OK, Maisie. Keep going. He's too busy digging his tractor out of the hedge to watch us.'

Janey hung on as they bounced across the furrowed ground. This didn't seem like a very sophisticated method of transport for spies. Satispying might be risky, but at least it was cool. This was just painful – and about to become more so for the horses in their way.

'Look out!' she yelled. 'You'll hit them! Look, wow – isn't that the horse my dad and I rode to escape the Sinerlesse?' It seemed a long time ago now, but the horse looked very familiar – ever more familiar as the people carrier bludgeoned its way across the field, straight towards the horse and the driving rain which enveloped it.

'Ah yes, well done, Janey. That's the one.' And Mrs Halliday pressed down on the accelerator.

'What are you doing? You'll kill it! You'll kill us! Stop!'

Janey closed her eyes as the horse's muzzle loomed at them through the windscreen, and waited for the bump. Instead, all she heard was Alfie tutting and a slight slurping sound as the car seemed to stick for a moment, then blast off again with all its previous speed and more.

She opened her eyes cautiously. 'Is the horse OK?'

Alfie was shaking his head at her. 'I know my mum's a bit mad sometimes, but do you seriously think she'd point the car at a real live horse? It's a hologram, you loon, to hide the SPIcamp.'

'Well, technically,' piped up G-Mamma, 'the horse is just the key – a SPIRIT, or SPI Retinal Image Transfer. It's the WUSS that hides the camp; that sucking feeling was us passing through the Weather-Using Site Shield.'

'The rain!' Janey registered that there was only bright sunshine around them now, and they were slowing down as they approached a series of military-looking buildings.

'That's right, Janey,' said Mrs Halliday, sweeping expertly into a parking space between two other identical people carriers. 'There's an enormous force field all around the camp, which looks to all intents and purposes like an isolated shower – to the untrained eye. You can only get through by driving straight at the right horse, or at whatever SPIRIT has been chosen as the key. And here we are!'

Janey clambered down from the car and helped G-Mamma out. Trouble jumped across to her shoulder, and together they looked around, unsure which way to go, until Alfie raised his arm to point at someone, and she knew instantly what to do.

'Dad!'

There stood her father, just in the doorway of what seemed to be the administration block. He looked as he had when she'd seen him last – tall, crinkle-edged brown eyes and a flashing film-star grin. Abe Rownigan spread his arms wide. 'Welcome to SPIcamp! Welcome!'

'Dad, you're here!' Janey let Trouble drop to the ground and took off at a run, racing Trouble towards her father's embrace. Trouble was faster and flung himself at the open arms of his beloved master, but Janey didn't slow. There was room for them both in that hug.

But then something very peculiar occurred. Trouble made contact with her father's chest and disappeared. And as Janey reached out for her father, she too shot straight through his body. Tripping over Trouble on the other side, she thudded to the ground on hands and knees and stopped, stunned.

'Janey, don't you get it?'

She turned around to see Alfie clambering out of her father's back, followed by Mrs Halliday and G-Mamma, who struggled through like a squeezed marshmallow. The whole spectacle of people walking through her father was quite disgusting. 'Of course,' she said bitterly, trying to hide her embarrassment, 'he's a hologram too. A . . . a SPIRIT. He's not really there. Just a movie of him.'

Mrs Halliday helped her to her feet. 'I'm not sure if he's a SPIRIT or a Retro-spectre – a sort of image made up of how someone looked in the past, although that's such a new development that I doubt it. Still, you'll find a lot of surprising things at this SPIcamp, Janey. That's why it will be so good for you – for all of us. We'll get to see what your father has been working on lately and receive the best training in the spying world. If he turns up in person, that will be an added bonus, won't it?'

Janey nodded, feeling dangerously close to tears. She'd hoped so much he was going to be there, and when she saw Abe standing there she'd believed her dreams had come true. Now she had to pull herself together and act like the spylet he would wish her to be. 'So, where do we go now?'

The hologram of her father turned around and gestured to a door at the back of the office. 'Through the Wower, SPI-friends, and on to the Briefing Room. Welcome, once again, to SPIcamp!'

Seconds later, they stepped out of the Wower stalls in full spy gear. Janey was now Jane Blonde, platinum ponytailed, Girl-gauntlet and Ultra-gogs at the ready, and glittering in her silver Lycra SPIsuit. Her cat, meanwhile, had become one hundred per cent spy-pet, with hypnotic green eyes, shimmering go-faster stripes down each side and a golden tail which he waggled around like a great fat ostrich feather. They regrouped on the way to the door marked 'Briefing Room'. Janey felt nervous, like she had on her first day at Winton School. This time, however, she knew each of the people standing with her was definitely friend not foe, and they all had her best interests at heart.

G-Mamma shifted the purple veil which descended from her gleaming lilac turban and whispered urgently to Janey. 'Now don't forget, Blondelicious – we're not sure who knows that Boz-Sol-Abe is your father, so let's keep that to ourselves. No more throwing yourself at his SPIRIT for huggy-wuggies.'

'Right,' said Janey, blushing. 'I promise.'

'Let's go,' said Alfie, up ahead of them.

He pushed open the door and they all trooped in, Janey clutching a quaffed and golden Trouble to her like a furry shield. The white domed room was half-full of people and completely devoid of anything else. Taking a quick glance around, Janey reckoned there were another four Spylets with their SPI:KEs: a tall girl in red, a bit younger than Janey, with bright auburn hair in feathery curls around her face, with a woman who looked like a taller version of her; a boy in a green padded SPIsuit like a racing driver's and a sleek helmet the colour of a holly leaf, with microphone attached, acompanied by an anxious, thin-haired man who kept twiddling the dial on his SPI-Pod; and a set of black-haired twins in SPIsuits as liquid and black as ink – one boy, one girl – who stood with cross faces and crossed arms on either side of their SPI:KEs – their parents, Janey guessed. They were obviously having a job keeping the twins apart.

'No other spy-pets,' she commented to Alfie.

Alfie looked at Trouble and laughed. 'How do they manage?'

She nudged him with her elbow. 'You're just jealous.' She knew he'd love a dog but wasn't allowed.

Janey, Alfie, G-Mamma and Mrs Halliday were just taking their place at the end of the line of Spylets and SPI:KEs when a chill wind whistled through the room. They all looked up to see the figure of Abe Rownigan floating above them, high up in the curve of the ceiling. A few of the strangers let out startled gasps. Abe smiled down at them and opened his arms as he had earlier, only this time Janey knew he wasn't inviting her in for a family reunion. She swallowed hard and waited for the SPIRIT to speak.

'Spies and Spylets, welcome to SPIcamp. I hope you'll forgive me for not being here in person but in, ahem, SPIRIT only. Perhaps you don't recognize me in my current guise. You will have believed, most of you, that your invitation came from Solomon Brown. I am Solomon Brown. Solomon Brown, however, is an invention: the made-up brother of a real SPI who you believed was dead . . . but who has actually survived all this time. I am Boz 'Brilliance' Brown, also known as Solomon Brown, and latterly the businessman Abe Rownigan.'

There was a pause while the other eight people in the room stared at each other open-mouthed and then turned suspiciously to Janey and her crew, who were not looking at all surprised by this news.

'How do we know this is not a trick?' The man in the green suit folded his arms as he gazed up at the figure fluttering against the roof.

'Good point. Let me give you some validations. Magenta and Titian Ambition, you've been responsible for covering European operations for six years, four months, and –' he checked his watch – 'thirteen days, since I bought out your excellent family ice-cream company.'

'Best in the west,' agreed the red-suited woman with a smile.

'And please call me Tish,' said the auburn-haired girl with a similar broad, gap-toothed grin.

'Tish it is. Now, Eagle and Peregrine,' said Abe, pointing to the parents of the twins, 'Japanese kite-riders supreme, until Eagle was shot with an air rifle by a curious kid.'

'What was the kid called?' said the father, testing.

'I believe you call him Rook these days.'

The boy in the black suit winced. 'You said that was our family secret!'

His father grinned. 'I only ever told one person: the boss.'

Abe turned his attention to the man who had asked for proof. 'And last but not least: Ivan Erikssen, with your son Leaf – I met you when working with Reg Baron. You were the first person to come up with the cell-tagging for the Crystal Clarification Process, and you discovered it because of your wife's sickle-cell disease.'

The man nodded slowly. 'I never told anybody else about that. You must be the genuine article . . . although you look a lot different to the spy I remember.'

'I can't afford, for your sake or mine, to appear to you in person,' explained the Abe SPIRIT, 'so you will have to make do with a holographic image controlled from a distance.'

'Can you hear us then,' shouted the boy twin rudely, 'or are you just like a DVD?'

Abe laughed. 'No, I can hear you, Rook. And see you! I see you and your twin, Blackbird, are getting on as well as ever.'

The boy chuckled, impressed, and uncrossed his arms for the first time. Now that Janey looked at them, the whole family looked rather bird-like, with long noses and arms, and minuscule feathers on their SPIsuits that shimmered in the shifting air.

'We should continue the introductions,' said Abe, pointing to Alfie. 'You may already have heard of the Hallidays, spy-names Halo and Al Halo. Halo . . . Maisie . . . is one of my most trusted colleagues. I hope you will learn from her as much as from your tutors. And finally, we have my . . . my personal and rather late selection for the world of spying, who is proving to be a formidable force.' Janey felt a blaze of warmth, even from the holographic brown eyes. 'Here, along with her inimitable SPI:KE G-Mamma, is Jane Blonde, Sensational Spylet.'

Janey stood, self-consciously staring at the SPIRIT to avoid the twins' look of cool appraisal, the raised eyebrow of Leaf and the frank, open stare of Tish. Suddenly the SPIRIT winked at her, and she laughed aloud in surprise. The message was clear: her dad might not be able to be there in person, but he was looking out for her, wherever he was.

'So, what are we doing here, sir?' said Leaf after a moment or two.

'Ah, first score to Leaf,' said Abe with a grin. 'Fairly important to establish why I'm dragging you away from your schooling to spend a week under a force field. Well, there are two reasons for asking you here. Three, perhaps, if I include the fact that some of you needed to know I'm still alive. Reason one: I've chosen you all for your incredible potential. I wanted the chance to test out your skills, and to give you all the chance to do some additional training, in a safe environment, before anything more threatening happens. Reason two: those of us who mean to carry on spying for the good of the world need to close ranks. I want you to get to know each other, be a team. I would trust each and every one of you with my life, and I want you all to know that you can do the same with each other.'

The reasons sounded credible, but somewhere between Janey's stomach and her chest there was a knot of something strange – the odd feeling that she had come to think of as her spy instinct. Something was missing.

She looked up. 'Um . . .' she said quietly, 'err . . . why?'

Silence cloaked them all instantly. Then Janey was very relieved to see that the wavering holographic image of her father was smiling. 'Ah yes,' he said. 'Well done, Janey. Why indeed? I've only told you the surface reasons why I want you to come here. What I haven't yet divulged is the underlying motivation for needing a crack team of spies, united in their fervour to do good.'

Janey knew instantly. 'It's Copernicus, isn't it?'

'No! Not my fa– not him again!' groaned Alfie.

With a sorrowful nod, Abe continued. 'Yes, it is Copernicus. Some of you may know this already; others will not. Copernicus has become a power-crazed madman. He will stop at nothing. Already he's turned the Sinerlesse Spy Group against us by persuading them that I was responsible for the death of their beloved family member Reg Baron. The spies who knew Copernicus as the Sun King have sought to reach us and kill us. He's even cloned our own spies. We thought we had him safely caged – frozen, in fact. But somehow he escaped, presumably because of another loyal fool who had been promised something impossibly grand in the world takeover Copernicus is planning. He's a very dangerous enemy, persuasive and influential, and he's regrouping. If he becomes an enemy with an army, we need to be able to fight back. You people are my own army.'

He waited a moment for the news to sink in. Alfie muttered inaudibly and popped a piece of gum in his mouth, a sure sign that he was nervous. Copernicus was not only an evil overlord, he was also Alfie's father, as the Spylet had almost let slip. As such, he knew that any suspicion of betrayal must first fall on him. His mum put an arm around him, and Janey gave him a small, lacklustre smile. G-Mamma, meanwhile, was blossoming like a sunflower. She loved nothing better than a good fight.

'So, my friends,' said Abe quietly, 'can I ask that of you? Are you ready for that?'

'Ready? Oh YEAH!' yelled G-Mamma, punching the air. 'Bring on those baddies and let's whup 'em good!

33

'We'll thrash 'em.
We'll mash 'em.
We'll round them up and bash 'em.
We'll stick them in
Our rubbish bin
And absolutely trash 'em.'

Those who didn't already know G-Mamma stared round-eyed at her jubilant outburst, and Janey managed to lay a hand on her SPI:KE's arm just before she started to whirl around doing a victory dance. 'Later,' she said quickly out of the corner of her mouth.

'Oh, sorree!' G-Mamma folded her arms sulkily and glared at Tish, who was covering her mouth with her scarlet Girl-gauntlet in an attempt to hide her laughter.

Abe laughed too. 'Janey's right, G-Mamma. We don't have the right to celebrate yet. At the present time we don't even know what we're up against. I know only this: Copernicus is a clever, devious enemy, with as much technical and scientific knowledge at his fingertips as I have. He's already discovered the secret of reincarnation and a key to evading death, and he can make infinite copies of his spies and his prisoners. Wherever he is, there is no end to his ambitions. So,' he said, rubbing his hands together, 'here's what SPIcamp will consist of. Each day you'll be doing physical training in the spy-sports hall, and catching up with our current technologies. You will also be set tasks by me. And these tasks must be carried out alone. Try to be creative – don't rely on the same gadgets and strategies all the time. I have to be sure that each of you is ready, and that I can trust you completely.'

Alfie cleared his throat self-consciously. 'Sir, do you mind me asking who our tutors are going to be?'

Abe smiled. 'Not at all. I told you in the invitation to the camp that I'd hand-picked both students and tutors. It might have been more honest to say that I *self*-picked the tutors. They are all me – all my SPIRITs. You'll find briefing packs with your timetables and maps of the grounds in the Spylab through that door behind Ivan.' They all turned to see a space where previously there had been a solid wall. 'Go through now, and everything will become clear as the week goes by. Oh, and this is very important – a good team plays together and eats together, so I've set up a restaurant on the site, where the best food will be available for breakfast, lunch and dinner—'

'Hallelujah!' yelled G-Mamma.

Abe laughed. '. . . PROVIDED you are all together. The divided team goes hungry.'

'You mean, kind of like *Survivor*?' said Tish with a grin, and those who had seen the reality TV show (which was everybody but Janey) laughed.

But the room fell silent as Abe's SPIRIT suddenly looked very serious. 'We are certainly in this for survival. But there is no competition among ourselves. Under this force field, there are no individual winners or losers. You are a team – one team. You stick together, or fall apart.'

There was a long pause while this sank in and the 'team' looked at each other sideways, wondering who might be the one to break the unit that Abe was trying to create. Janey knew that trust needed to be earned – by now she had enough experience of people who appeared to be allies but turned out to be quite the opposite. As she glanced around she saw that a few pairs of eyes were fixed stonily on Alfie.

This week was not going to be the holiday camp they had imagined.

satispies and spyroscopes

It was still only mid-morning, just a couple of hours after they'd arrived, but with the lights off and the blackout blinds in operation, Janey couldn't even see her hand in front of her face. The feeling was very disorientating. She'd been sent into a blackout room to be introduced to a new gadget, shoving her way through the airlock at the door, and she didn't really feel that she ought to make use of her old SPI-buys. But the darkness was closing in oppressively, pushing at her temples, squeezing the breath out of her . . .

'Oh, forget hanging on,' she muttered to Trouble, who was squirming around her Fleet-feet, rattling the bell on his collar to make his presence felt. Presumably he could see better than she could, but even he didn't seem keen to move. With her left hand, she squeezed the ring finger on her Girl-gauntlet, releasing a laser of light, and directed it at Trouble's tail. In his Wowed state, his tail lit up like a beacon when the laser danced off the golden fur, and light bounced out in a one-metre circle around the spy duo.

Janey gulped. She appeared to be suspended in mid-air. She couldn't see where the bottom of the room was, but she could hear that though the atmosphere around her was still, the air around the room's perimeter was rushing and gushing like a whirlwind. It reminded her of the gusty tornadoes that had been sparked off whenever Copernicus (disguised as Abe Rownigan) set the SPI-clone off to make a copy of something – or someone. 'I hope I'm not being cloned,' she said out loud, rather more bravely than she felt.

At once there was a laugh, and the room filled with light as a hundred tiny bulbs peppered the roof like stars. 'No, but it's the same principle,' said the Abe-SPIRIT who was now hovering directly across the room from her, unaffected by the roaring wind. She still had to fight the temptation to run across and give him a hug – though what she would actually run *on* she had no idea.

'Like with the SPI-clone,' her father was explaining, 'the use of the vortex is all important. You might know that the centre of a cyclone or tornado is very still. In this case, we've created a fixed vortex and suspended you in the middle of it. That's why you had to push through at the door. It's a Spyroscope – useful for getting you out of harm's way. When you're in the middle of the vortex it's very difficult to reach you, with bullets, hands or blades.'

Janey nodded. 'But I can't carry a room like this around in my SPIsuit, can I?'

'Ah,' said Abe. 'No, you can't. But hold on to Trouble for a moment . . .'

She did, grasping his collar with its collection of bells and tags and holding her breath as the roar of the wind started to die down. 'I'm sinking!' she cried. It wasn't unpleasant, but she was definitely dropping, heading for the floor of the vast, tank-like room.

'You just switched it off,' explained her father's SPIRIT.

'But . . . how?' Janey patted her way up and down her SPIsuit. She had on her Girl-gauntlet and a SuSPInder belt. Her ASPIC (which appeared to be a skateboard but was actually an Aeronautical SPI Conveyor) was strapped to her thigh, and there was even a small chunk of SPInamite tucked into a pocket on her sleeve – definitely for advanced Spylets only. There was nothing new there. Nor was there anything to be found in her high platinum ponytail or her narrow, letter-box-shaped Ultra-gogs. 'I don't understand.'

Her father crossed his arms and gazed at her expectantly. 'OK, I have to work it out,' she said after a moment. 'Is it something I activated when I walked into the room? No, that wouldn't be it, because it needs to be something portable. So what else . . . hang on a minute.'

She looked down at her Spycat, who was

busily licking at his paws and dragging them through his quiff, his cat-bell dinging madly whenever he waggled his head. 'Since when does Trouble have a bell?'

A broad smile spread over her father's face. 'Exactly. What he has now is a Spyroscope that looks to all intents and purposes like a small glass bell, such as you might see on any domestic cat. You just need to enclose it in the palm of your hand to activate it, and again to deactivate. Of course, this time we activated it for you, but you turned it off yourself by grabbing it.'

'Clever.' Janey could see how the Spyroscope might be very useful in certain situations.

'Janey,' said her father, a new tone entering his voice, 'I've gathered you all together and am starting to introduce new gadgets like the Spyroscope because sinister things are happening . . .'

Now he had all of Janey's attention. 'Like what?'

The SPIRIT scratched his head. 'It's not all easy to explain. There's nothing actually wrong in some instances, but my instincts are telling me that something's amiss. You'll understand that, Janey. But some of the evidence is very tangible. You know we kept all the spies we've thwarted in our recent missions frozen in our secret hideout?'

'The one that's so secret nobody but you knows where it is?'

'So I thought,' said the Abe-SPIRIT seriously.

'But someone else must have found out. All the spies have been broken out of captivity.'

Janey swallowed. 'Sounds like Copernicus. I know I sort of blew him up, but I knew even that might not have finished him off.' She'd hoped that when she planted SPInamite in the Wower containing Copernicus he'd disappear for ever, but of course his cells were traceable if enough bits of him were rescued by his cohorts. There was always a chance that he might be reformed.

'That's what I suspect,' agreed her father. 'I'm particularly suspicious about him, as two of my agents, who were operating as scientists at the secret location, have been found dead. They . . . they had both been crushed. The life was literally squeezed out of them.'

'Oh no. Oh, Dad,' whispered Janey. 'That's terrible. This is getting really serious.'

'Precisely.'

'And what's the part you can't really explain?'

Her father rubbed his chin. 'It's the animals that live around the location of my secret facility. They're all acting very out of sorts. They're skittish and restless. I know their strange behaviour means something, but I don't know what.'

He looked at Trouble as he spoke, and Janey recalled the strong bond that Abe had always had with his cat. Trouble had been able to pick him out even when he was Crystal Clarified into another form, and the cat could tell when someone who looked exactly like him was actually an imposter. Animals acted on instinct, Janey knew, and that was incredibly important in their line of work too.

'We'll work it out, Dad,' she said softly.

He looked up, distracted. 'Yes. Yes, of course we will.'

Janey paused. She really wanted to warn her father that Jean was on the hunt for a new boyfriend, but he looked so worried that she couldn't bring herself to tell him. She would have to deal with that one herself.

Just then the Abe-SPIRIT lifted his head, putting his worries aside. 'We'll try to find time to talk some more during the week, Janey, but you'll have to appreciate that we're on a very tight schedule, with a great deal to do. Obstacle course after lunch.' And with that the SPIRIT of her father blew her a kiss and evaporated.

'Bye, Dad. Oh! How do I . . . ?'

Janey took in her surroundings for the first time. She was inside a huge cube, with the only door halfway up the wall. When she'd made her way into the room she'd been hovering on a cushion of air on a level with the door, but now it was a good few metres away. This was clearly another test. 'Fleet-feet won't jump that far, Twubs,' she said. 'I think it might be time to try out that bell again.'

She gripped the little globe on Trouble's collar and

felt it open like a flower under her palm. Through her fingers a breeze tickled, turning quickly into a whistling gale that forced her hand open. Then the Spyroscope began its work in earnest, whipping the air around them into a frenzy while cocooning them in a protective cushion of air on which they rose twenty or thirty feet until they were once again suspended in the middle of the room. Turning towards the door, Janey leaned her sharp ponytail into the wind, the better to slice her way through, and with Trouble hanging on to her leg she battled her way through the stormy wind zone at the edge of the room to the door, walking on air, and tugged on the handle.

Suddenly she was outside the vortex room. 'Phew,' she said, smoothing out Trouble's quiff as she spotted someone approaching. It was good to be on solid ground again. 'Alfie! What have you been doing?'

'Advanced Boy-battler,' said her friend, showing her the new black glove on his right hand. He looked incredibly pleased with it. 'Rocket launcher, dragnet, video projector and a totally cool acid spray gun that would melt through a bank vault. That's in this finger . . . or, no, whoops, which one was it?'

Janey watched him jabbing at his glove with his left hand. 'I think you'd better get that right before you do some damage. What have you got next?'

Alfie pointed with his middle finger, and immediately his timetable was projected on to the wall. 'Um, nothing until after lunch. But that's only half an hour away.'

'Me too,' said Janey, a plan formulating in her mind. 'Look, there's something I really need to do back at home. Can you help me?'

Alfie raised an eyebrow. 'You heard Abe. If we miss lunch, we're in big trouble.'

'I just want you to press the Satispy control. There must be one around here.'

'Oh no. You know I hate that thing.'

'But it's really important! My mum might be in trouble. You know I'd help you and your mum if you needed it.'

That much was certainly true. Alfie wrestled with his conscience for a few moments, then shrugged. 'All right, but if you're not back for lunch, don't tell anyone I was involved.'

Janey grinned as she reached over to Trouble's collar. 'I will be. It's just a little idea I had. Something I have to do.' She'd already realized she had to deal with her 'mum' problem herself. Best to get in right at the beginning, before the planning had even started.

They located the Satispy control in the administration outbuilding, where they'd first met Abe the SPIRIT. 'Makes sense,' said Alfie. 'This must be where they organize all the visitors and what have you.'

'Just give me ten minutes and then bring me back,

OK?' Janey slipped the Spyroscope off Trouble's collar and pocketed it, and prepared for the stomach-lurching journey.

Alfie checked his watch and then, a little reluctantly, pressed the button on the Satispy activator. Janey watched him disappear as her eyeballs separated and she streamed up to the nearest satellite station. Within seconds she was reassembling in her own back garden. She scooted down the side path to the front of the house and flung herself into G-Mamma's unruly front yard.

'Just in time,' she said as a smart black hatchback pulled up at the gate. Taking the Spyroscope out of her pocket, Janey crouched behind G-Mamma's hedge and waited for Joy, the administrator from Abe 'n' Jean's Clean Machines, to step up the path. She was dressed in her Sunday best, in a summery skirt and T-shirt. Her mum was opening the door, smiling in welcome. 'Now!' said Janey sternly, and she gripped the Spyroscope firmly in her palm.

The whistling sensation prickled her palm, and she released the mini-tornado across the garden. Suddenly Joy found her freshly washed hair standing in a crest across the top of her head, her necklace whipping backwards and forwards across her face and her whole body pressed back against the gate she had just passed through, as she battled to keep her floaty skirt in place. Janey glanced at her mum; she

45

was hanging on to the door frame with both hands, trying to stop her feet from parting company with the doorstep. Although sounds were muffled around Janey, she could see the two women trying to shout to each other, the words being snatched from their mouths and thrown up into the sky like autumn leaves.

What she had forgotten, however, was that setting off the Spyroscope caused a huge globe of wind in which she would be suspended at the very central point. As the wind grew more furious between Joy and her mother, she felt herself rising up from behind the hedge, heading for the power lines above G-Mamma's roof.

'Oh no! They'll see me any second!' Janey looked around frantically. If she dropped the Spyroscope, the wind would drop too. If she didn't, she'd loom up next to them – or possibly even over them - like a SPIsuited phantom. 'Blonde, you idiot!'

'You said it.' A voice suddenly sounded close to her ear. Janey whipped around, and there, sitting on the edge of the roof behind the sycamore, was Titian Ambition.

'If you don't make it to lunch, Blonde, we're all history.' The red-haired girl glared at her belligerently.

'How did you get here?' gasped Janey. 'You're in my vortex!'

'I did my Spyroscope training just now, and when I noticed Al Halo lurking in the admin block I thought

I'd better check up on you both. I've brought the remote control for the Satispy. Time to go back to camp.'

'But my . . .' Janey looked down from where they were hovering next to G-Mamma's chimney. Her mother had slammed the door and Joy was struggling back to her car. Success.

Not that Tish waited to hear about it. Without warning or apology, she pointed the remote control at Janey and pressed, and suddenly the wind dropped away, and then the garden, and then the Earth, until Janey was suddenly splatting back down near the administration block, with Titian Ambition mere seconds behind her, and a bevy of SPI:KEs stalking across to the refectory with very cross faces.

tumble-tubes

Janey and Tish skidded up to the door of the refectory several minutes after the rest of the SPIs.

'See?' said Tish with a flick of her head. 'One more minute of your tornado time and we'd have been toast.'

G-Mamma looked at Janey, puzzled. 'What were you up to, Blondette? You nearly made me miss my lunch.'

'I . . . I was worried about my mum,' said Janey.

'She set off a Spyroscope right next to her,' blurted Tish in her surprisingly loud voice. 'How worried is that?'

'That sounds very odd, Janey,' said Mrs Halliday, somehow commanding Janey to explain herself without raising her voice. Alfie twitched uncomfortably.

Janey sighed. She didn't really want to be telling everyone her family's private business. 'It's nothing really. Just . . . some family stuff.'

Magenta put out her hand so that Tish trotted to her side. 'Well, thankfully my Titian Ambition was there to sort it out. It appears to me no harm's been done. But there will be if we all stand around chatting about it.'

The other SPI:KEs considered this for a moment and then nodded their agreement. Janey, Alfie and even Tish breathed a sigh of relief and followed the adults into the refectory. 'Good start,' the girl muttered softly in Janey's ear. 'Keep this up and you won't be "sensational" for much longer.'

Janey glowered at Tish's scarlet back as she stalked off in front of her. For someone even younger than Janey, she was very sure of herself, and not a little competitive. Titian Ambition was the right name for her, and she was definitely someone to be watched, Janey decided. She just wasn't sure what she should be watching her for.

In the refectory, G-Mamma had stationed herself at the head of the table and was handing round the serving dishes that were perched on slender stainless-steel tripods, being sure to dollop a huge mound of everything on to her own plate first. Soon everyone was tucking into sausage and mash with fresh peas and broccoli, followed by apple crumble with a choice of custard or cream. Janey wasn't particularly hungry and pushed a sausage round her plate, trying not to feel too guilty about almost getting them all into trouble.

It didn't work, and the horrible anxious feeling in her stomach seemed to fill her to bursting.

Everyone else was soon bursting too. 'If they keep feeding us like this, I'm going to need a bigger SPIsuit,' said Peregrine half an hour later, snapping the black-feathered Lycra against her taut stomach as the dishes were automatically replenished once again.

'Bring it on,' beamed G-Mamma, happily helping herself to a second portion of crumble with custard, cream, a sausage and a bit more cream. 'We obviously need to keep our strength up.'

'That's right,' said Abe suddenly, and they all turned to see a SPIRIT standing at the far end of the table. 'You might need a couple of extra layers in the near future. And you're going to be doing some hard physical work during the next week, so be sure to eat well. You have ten minutes before I need you all at the obstacle course.'

Janey was looking forward to the obstacle course. Throughout her missions she had always been able to use her SPI-buys to good effect to get out of, into, over or under things, and she imagined this was going to be no different. Hastily shoving her plate to one side, she joined the queue at the door and jogged behind Eagle and his son Rook to the obstacle-course zone. G-Mamma lagged behind, groaning roundly, until she thought to pop the wheels out of her in-line skate-shoes and roll her way to the site.

'Is this it?' Janey looked around at the field at which they'd arrived. She'd expected an army obstacle course, with tall wooden structures, flying foxes and perhaps the odd chain of tyres to run through, but there was nothing like that. This field had a high fence around the edge, with a sturdy gate to one side, and was simply divided into four by a couple of large fences criss-crossing in the middle. Surely that wasn't all they'd be expected to do – leap over a few fences? That could be done with a straightforward Fleet-feet jump. Leaf, who was standing beside her, shrugged as his eyes flicked backwards and forwards. 'I am sure that Mr Rownigan has something planned for us. We just have to wait and see.'

There was nothing else for it. Janey stood around, trying to catch Alfie's eye to see if they could pair up, but he seemed engrossed in conversation with Leaf's father and didn't make eye contact. In fact, everyone was talking intently with someone new – G-Mamma to Peregrine, Mrs Halliday to Titian Ambition, Ivan to Rook – and Janey suddenly felt rather left out. It was with some relief, then, that she saw the Abe-SPIRIT at the gateway to the field.

He pointed to the locked entrance. 'One at a time, please. Find your way in, tackle each quarter in order and run through me at the end to record your time. And remember what I said earlier – try not to use the same trick twice.'

The spies jumped quickly into line. Tish was first – no surprise there, thought Janey. Miss Know-it-all. The redhead stood in front of the gate, looked puzzled for a few moments as Abe spoke to her, then tapped something into a small keypad by the entrance. The gateway slid open and Tish disappeared. Behind her went Magenta, listening intently to the SPIRIT and then pondering for some time at the gateway before finally throwing her head back in realization and punching the keypad.

The line moved slowly, Janey at the back. As she watched she noticed that a pattern was emerging: all the SPI:KEs were taking much longer than the Spylets to go through. G-Mamma, in particular, kept talking back at Abe and spent ages trying to key in the right code until she finally gave up and shuffled to the back of the queue behind Janey.

'Blasted codes,' she cursed as she passed. 'Couldn't he just give me someone to pulverize?'

Suddenly it was Janey's turn. She walked up to her father, who simply smiled at her and said, 'See you, mate.'

It sounded slightly odd – he usually called her 'darling' or 'sweetheart' or just 'Janey' – but she smiled back anyway. 'Thanks, Dad. See you soon.'

He simply nodded and remained still, staring at her . . . and suddenly she got it. He hadn't said goodbye at all. He'd been giving her the code. It was just like a text message – the Spylets were getting it more quickly because they were more familiar with mobile phones! G-Mamma relied on Janey for all the code-cracking and would never get this, so she hoped fervently that her SPI:KE was still wearing her SPI-Pod. With a hand poised over the keyboard, she spoke each keystroke aloud as if she was concentrating. 'See you, mate. So . . . C . . . U . . . M . . . 8.'

There was a tiny whoop of 'Cody crafty!' behind her, signalling to her that G-Mamma had indeed been wearing her listening device, and then the gate slid open. She stepped through into the grassy pasture and took another step forward as the gate slid home behind her. So far, so good. She took another step . . . and found herself up to her knees in mud. Furthermore, there was a sucking sensation beneath her feet, which reminded her of a scene from a film she'd watched with Alfie. The baddy had been gobbled up by the ground. 'It's a bog!'

She frantically thought through her options as the peaty earth swallowed her further until her knees, thighs and then her hips were fully submerged. There was nothing to push against to activate her Fleet-feet, and she was trapped almost to her waist so the ASPIC strapped to her thigh was useless. She forced herself to remember not to struggle, as that would pull her in further, but it didn't seem to be making much difference; the bog sucked her in anyway. Her own father was about to kill her. He would have to dig her out of a sloppy, muddy grave, only to put her back in another one after he'd explained to her mum what he'd done. The holes in the SuSPInder around her waist made tiny bubbles in the mud, like the little air bubbles her own mouth would make when she was pulled right under . . .

And then it came to her. 'SuSPInder! Of course.' Before it disappeared into the mire completely, Janey grabbed the buckle of the belt and unwound it. Coiling it like a lasso above her head, and trying to ignore the thick mud that had now reached almost to her shoulders, she flung the buckle towards the fence at the far side of the bog. Like a grappling hook the buckle caught, and Janey yanked on the line suspended from the fence to her boggy body until it tightened. With a nasty slurp she was pulled from the earth, dragged across the deceptively grassy surface of the bog and hoisted up the fence. She sat there for a moment, gathering her breath before she dropped down into the next segment of field, just as she heard the gate slide shut behind G-Mamma followed by a ferocious yelp as the bog took a hold. 'You let go of me now, boggy bog, or you'll be sorry!'

Janey grinned as she glanced around at her new obstacle. Once again it appeared simply to be a quarter of a field, with a tall fence on every side. The fences were taller here than in the previous section though.

Janey looked again. They looked taller still. But they weren't actually taller, she realized. They were closer. With every passing second they got a bit nearer to her. They were boxing her in. And fast. She patted the SPInamite in her pocket. Should she blast a way through them? It might work, but the fences were closing in so quickly she might not have time. Suddenly they were just an arm's length away . . . moving in to flatten her . . .

The move she made had almost become second nature. Bracing her arms against the walls encroaching on her, she drew up her feet and banged them down as hard as she could. The Fleet-feet exploded into operation and she sprang into the sky, sailing upwards like a firework and coming to land on the very tops of the fences as they finally drew together. To her shock, Janey found that they weren't just simple white wooden fences. Behind each one a solid block of granite was now apparent. Each block had shifted across the field so that Janey now stood atop a great platform of grey stone. All she had to do now was walk across it, vault down and land in field three.

Only she didn't exactly land. As her feet touched the grass, the ground parted beneath her feet and Janey found herself sinking into murky cold water. Instantly she groped in her sleeve pocket for a small rubber device and shoved it between her teeth. The SPIder sent two legs out between her lips and up her nose, then anchored the remaining six legs around her mouth and shot oxygen down her throat. It was much easier to work out what to do when you could breathe, as Janey had discovered before.

'Hmm, mucky, but nothing dangerous,' she decided as she peered into the water through her Ultra-gogs. She worked out which was the far side of the field and then swam towards it. 'Ah.'

So this was the real test. The sides of the field were completely sheer. She came up against the fence and swam to the surface, but there was no foothold to help her up and over the wall. Perhaps she wasn't in the right spot? But as Janey looked around she could see that every fence was exactly the same – smooth and impenetrable. Behind, G-Mamma was pounding across the granite platform, heading in Janey's direction.

Which gave her an idea.

OK, Blonde, she thought. If you can't climb it, ride it. Groping under the water, Janey unstrapped her ASPIC from her leg and settled it on the surface. Then, with her stomach flat against the board and her limbs over the edge, as she had seen surfers do on TV, she paddled the ASPIC over to the middle of the field. From there she shouted at G-Mamma to jump in beside her. Seconds later there was an almighty plop. Janey hung on to her board and waited, and suddenly she was riding high on a great wave that took her above the top of the fence. As the wave curled over into a muddy crest, she clambered upright. Her Fleet-feet magnetically gripped on to the ASPIC and, whooping joyfully, she flew over the top of the fence like a champion surfer and straight down the other side, landing just a couple of centimetres from the wall. As the wave slapped against the fence, it surged back to G-Mamma, who was poised to follow her Spylet's example. 'Go, Blonde-girl,' she hollered.

'Easy-peasy.' Janey jumped off her board on to the grass of the fourth field and strapped it back in place against her leg. She was starting to enjoy herself. She'd been able to use all her familiar gadgets and hadn't even had too much thinking to do. The only SPI-buy she hadn't yet used was her SPInamite, so she eased it out of her pocket and held it tight as she waited for the final obstacle.

Stepping forward carefully, she nudged the ground with her toe. It seemed solid enough. Janey trod more confidently, then paused. The fences seemed to be getting taller again. Surely her father wouldn't try the same trick twice? If he had, she'd have to think harder about getting out of it, as she didn't want to use the Fleet-feet jump again. But no, this time was different. The two side fences were curving around her. The far fence had slid down across the grass towards her, also bending, so that it fitted between the two arced side panels. And as she looked up, the fence behind her was sliding over her head in a vast arch like

57

the roof of a cathedral. Suddenly there was a great snapping sound and the four bowed panels clunked together to form a long cylinder, with Janey at one end and, she could see now, her father at the other. She smiled and moved towards him.

And the nightmare began.

The cylinder started to turn. Janey toppled over, crunching her shoulder against the sides, then rode up helplessly towards the top of the spinning tube and fell back down again. It was like being inside a huge washing machine. The fences were just a white blur as they spun around and around, churning Janey up and tossing her against the sides. Unable to find her footing, she was completely at the mercy of this revolving monster, unclear which way was forward and which back, with no idea how to get a foothold, stand up, reach her father . . .

Janey felt incredibly sick. The motion was constant, dizzying. She couldn't even drop to her knees and crawl. As the white walls of the tube started to judder up and down before her eyes, she knew that the blurring was something to do with her brain, not with the tube itself. She was going to faint, and then she'd be left to be tossed around in there like a dead hamster in some grotesque hamster wheel.

There was only one thing left to try. She'd blow her way out.

And just as she struggled to guide the SPInamite

into her mouth, screaming as her limbs banged relentlessly against the unforgiving trap, the whiteness of her prison exploded before her eyes into deep, deep black, and she realized the screaming was not her, not her at all, but a ghost . . . a SPIRIT . . . her father.

6 titian ambition

Janey woke up to someone rudely poking around in her mouth with a sharp-nailed finger.

'No, that's all of it,' she heard G-Mamma say. 'No more stuck in her teeth or anything, so we don't need to worry about exploding fillings.'

Exploding fillings, thought Janey dreamily. Now *that* could be a good idea. Just as she was wondering whether she had inherited her father's ability to invent gadgets, she realized what G-Mamma had been doing and sat up with a start. Several faces were staring down at her, perturbed, while one or two, notably Tish and Rook, were looking a little smug. Her eyes found her father's SPIRIT, leaning over her with a hard-to-read expression.

'Did I blast my way out of that awful spinning tube?' she said weakly. A wave of nausea rose from her stomach just thinking about it, and she swallowed hard.

60

And at that Abe sat down and grabbed hold of her, squeezing her tight against his chest. 'No, Janey. You nearly blew yourself to pieces, and I nearly lost my daughter. You were too disorientated – you'd never have got the SPInamite out of your mouth and on to the tube and then got sufficiently out of the way in time. I never imagined it would affect you – any of you – as badly as that. Oh, Janey.'

Janey looked up at her father's grey face. 'I'd have been fine . . .'

'You'd have been Janey jam,' said G-Mamma firmly.

Abe shook his head, gripping her shoulders, hardly able to speak. 'If G-Mamma hadn't heard my scream, run into the tube and slapped you on the back so hard the SPInamite flew out of your mouth, you wouldn't be here now.'

Janey's shoulders slumped. This was bewildering. She'd nearly died and . . . she'd failed. She'd flunked one of her father's tests. 'It was all the spinning, and the whiteness. I didn't know which way to go. I thought . . .'

She had to stop as a burning sensation ripped across the bridge of her nose. She was going to cry. Bundled up in her dad's embrace, she was very, very tempted to let out the torrent of tears aching to be released.

But then Alfie waggled her foot with his. 'You weren't the only one who couldn't do it. It was like the worst fairground ride I've ever been on. I vommed all over Blackbird as I got out.'

Blackbird's sharp little face loomed into view. 'And he only did that because I was lying on the ground sobbing. It was the most horrible test of all, JB. Don't feel bad about it.'

But at least you made it out before you collapsed, thought Janey, and when she looked around at the others, at Leaf, Tish and Rook, she knew that they had skipped through it with no difficulties at all. It was exactly as Tish had said. She wasn't so sensational, after all.

Her father planted a kiss on her head. 'All right now? Perhaps you could try standing up.' And he got to his feet and stretched out a hand.

It was only as she took the proffered hand and stood up that Janey realized something. 'Dad, I can . . . I can feel you. You're solid.'

He smiled at Janey. 'Yes, it's me. Actually me. I've been operating all the holograms – the SPIRITS – from one central location on the camp. It allows me to be in several places at once and to appear in person from time to time if needs be. When I saw what was happening, I just . . .' He broke off, his jaw working furiously and his fingers pinching the top of his nose, and for the first time Janey knew why she got – used to get – that peculiar feeling whenever she was about to cry. It was inherited.

62

'So that's how SPIRITs and . . .' What was that other word Mrs Halliday had used? '. . . Retro-spectres work? You appear in a hologram but can come out in person?'

'Only SPIRITs work that way,' said her father. 'They're based on something real and current. Retro-spectres are built out of past memories and images, so can never appear in flesh and blood. But I'm very real, Janey. And, thank the heavens, so are you.'

Taking a deep breath, Abe called the spy group to him. 'That was a tough test. You all did amazingly well. G-Mamma, I'll never be able to thank you enough for your quick reactions.'

'I know – talk about speedy!' yelled G-Mamma, her eyes round with amazement at her own super-skills. 'I should change my name to G-Force! Oh yeah!

'G-Force . . . of course,
The speeeeeeed of a jet,
G-Force . . . racehorse,
The beeeeeeest you've met.'

'Modest, isn't she?' said Magenta pointedly, batting her eyelashes innocently as G-Mamma glared at her.

'Well, I for one have had enough excitement for one day,' said Abe. 'Even raps are a bit too much for me at the moment. You should all have some dinner, make any phone calls you need to make

– use the untraceable mobiles you'll find on each of your beds – and then turn in early. You've still got a week of challenges ahead of you, and you've seen now how serious they are.'

Janey loitered behind as the others started through the trees towards the refectory. 'You too, Janey,' he said. 'You'll need something to eat after that shock.'

'But can't I come with you?'

Abe shook his head. 'No. I'm sorry, Janey. You're here as a spy, not as my daughter, and you need to be part of that team. I'm sorry I had to reveal to you that I'm really here – I know how hard that's going to make it for you.'

It really was. The father she had missed so much was just seconds away all the time she was at the camp, and yet it seemed Janey could only be with him in snatched moments. Once again she felt her personalities stretching apart like a piece of elastic – on one end Jane Blonde, Spylet, and on the other Janey Brown, daughter. Why did she have to keep choosing?

Her father must have read her mind. He put a hand on each of her shoulders and gazed into her face. 'It means so much to me that you're here, Janey. Please try to keep yourself safe. And . . . make sure you ring Gina, I mean, your mum.'

And then he turned and strode away into the copse of trees, leaving Janey alone, and cold inside. She stomped sulkily over to her bed, picked up the mobile and keyed in the number. 'Hi, Mum,' she said. 'Are you OK?'

'Sweetheart! I'm fine. How are you? How's camp?'

It's awful, Janey wanted to wail. I'm no good at things and I've been in trouble already for trying to stop your dating plans, and my dad's here but I have to be a spy and not a daughter, and there are these smug Spylets who can do everything . . . 'Yes. Fine,' she said. 'Er, fun even.'

'Oh, good. Call me lots and lots, whenever you can find a minute. I expect you're going for dinner soon.'

'Yes, dinner's ready, I think,' said Janey, almost dropping the phone in panic. Dinnertime – and she wasn't there! The others would be furious. 'I'll try to call tomorrow. Bye, Mum.'

And almost before her mother had managed to answer, Janey ended the call and raced off to the refectory just in time. She grabbed a plate as G-Mamma finished piling beef bourgignon on to the last of the dishes. Janey held hers out expectantly. If spying and teamwork were what she was here for, then spying and teamwork were what she would do. Starting right now.

So for the rest of the week, Janey concentrated on being the best Spylet she possibly could. She found, as ever, that she excelled at the cryptology – deciphering codes and working out what secret messages meant. She zipped through the special puzzle-labyrinth, with its dingbats and cryptic messages, with barely a hiccup, putting jigsaws together, cracking codes in seconds and immediately spotting irregularities that showed the code was a booby trap.

Janey was also, and always had been, very quick thinking. When she found herself facing a ferocious bear in one of the challenges, for instance, she threw a Spyroscope into its open mouth. 'It's a robot!' she called to Tish, who was partnering her on the mission. 'Look at how jerky its movements are. It'll just fill up like a helium balloon.'

They watched as the bear burped loudly, inflated at a rate of knots and then floated into the air like a bear-shaped zeppelin. Tish, for once, had something complimentary to say to Janey, not least because she was the one the bear had been about to eat. 'Quick and effective, Blonde. Not pretty, but clever thinking. I'd have been robobear chow by now.'

Janey stared at her, surprised. 'That's the first nice thing you've ever said to me.'

'That's the first decent thing you've done,' said Tish, slowly lasering open the cage door to their gladiator-like challenge room with her scarlet Girl-gauntlet. The Gauntlets had now been upgraded, and featured titanium cutters instead of a pen, and a tiny heat-seeking missile where the camera had been. Tish grinned. 'Apart from having Abe as your dad. He's neat.'

'You might not be so sure if he was your dad. Hidden away all the time. Not able to spend time with you, even when you're in the same place. It has its drawbacks.' Janey Fleet-footed alongside Tish towards the Abe-SPIRIT that was recording their challenge-times.

'Oh no,' said Tish, shaking her auburn curls so hard she looked like a chrysanthemum. 'That man saved my life. There is nothing I wouldn't do for him, and if he was my dad I'd make sure he knew every second of every day how much I appreciated him.'

'He knows!' Janey was getting a little annoyed with Tish's hectoring tone. 'Anyway, what do you mean – he saved your life?'

'Dragged me out of a mine when I was kidnapped as a toddler. He somehow found out where I was, fought off all the bad guys and then got me out of a hundred-metre vertical shaft,' said Tish, panting slightly. 'My hero.'

'And mine,' said Janey under her breath, feeling a huge surge of daughterly pride.

Abe's SPIRIT was within sprinting distance now. Their time was going to be good. Suddenly though, and without warning, Tish operated her Fleet-feet jump and, with one smooth leap, ploughed up to the SPIRIT a good five seconds before Janey.

'I win,' she said with a small smile.

'But I saved you from being eaten!'

'You should have saved yourself from being beaten.' Tish smirked. 'You're way too nice.'

Annoyed, Janey decided that she really did not like Tish. About the others she was not so sure. Leaf appeared overly formal but otherwise all right, although he was so thin and fair he looked as if a strong wind would blow him over. No wonder he hadn't been trained to use a Spyroscope. Blackbird seemed particularly sweet – too sweet, especially in contrast to her big-headed brother, Rook, who outclassed everyone in the physical challenges and never lost a chance to gloat – almost as loudly as G-Mamma. Janey was so happy Alfie was with her. She loved the way he shone at everything but shrugged it all off as if he was merely doing what was expected of him.

The last day of camp came around just as Janey was starting to enjoy it – the new gadgets, the learning, getting to know other Spylets and SPI:KEs, who understood what it was like to lead a weird double life. Her father had appeared in person the previous night and spoken to her quietly. 'The biggest challenge, and the most relevant, is tomorrow, but I don't want you to do anything heroic just because you're my daughter and you have to prove yourself.'

Janey shook her head. 'I take risks because I'm a Spylet. That's what I'm here for, isn't it?'

'That's right,' said Abe solemnly. 'Well, all I can do is wish you good luck.' And he'd hugged her before disappearing into the dusk once more.

So here they were. The final challenge. Alfie raised one eyebrow at Janey as they made their way over to the designated zone. It was a vast dome that had been constructed behind the trees, hidden away where nobody had seen it before. Around the perimeter were twenty or so enormous generators – holding the dome up with air or something, Janey supposed. Abe (the real one, Janey felt, although she couldn't know for sure) stood before a small sealed doorway, rubbing his hands together.

'You have all come such a long way this week. I'm proud to have you on my side, and that's where I need you in these dangerous times. This is the most difficult test, the one that will decide who comes with me to my secret facility for the main part of this mission. Some of the test may look familiar, but please don't be fooled. Your previous tricks may work, but don't take them for granted. Be vigilant.' He looked around at the serious faces. 'You're ready. Good. The rules are: enter the code, complete each quarter in turn and run to me to record your time when you're done.'

Then he stepped away from the door, and Janey's heart sank. This sounded like the field challenge she'd found so difficult. Surely though, after the week's training she'd had, she'd be able to cope this time?

She waited for the line to dwindle, letting everyone go in ahead of her until she was the only one left.

'You'll be late,' said her father sternly, pointing at the gate.

Why's he being so bossy? thought Janey . . . Then she laughed. Of course. The code. She tapped in 'UL B L8' and looked back at her dad as the door swung open ahead of her. He nodded his encouragement, and she stepped into the dome.

snowdome

It was icy. Beyond icy. The temperature plummeted way below freezing the moment the door closed behind her. She had been in cold conditions before, but this compared only with when she'd been trapped in a freezer by the Sinerlesse. Her Blonde SPIsuit protected her body from her neck to her toes, but within seconds her face burned from the icy air, and her bare left hand felt withered and useless, the knuckles seizing up with the cold. She couldn't even see in the harsh white glare that bounced off the ground, the walls and the ceiling of the snowdome.

'Move, Blonde!' said Janey, urging herself to take action. Just standing there would be the worst possible thing to do; the icy temperatures would take hold in seconds . . . As quickly as she could with her numbed fingers, Janey wrapped her ponytail around her mouth and nose and tucked the end back into the band that held it in place. Now she had a loose mask covering the lower half of her face, below her Ultra-gogs. 'Far wall,' she instructed the glasses. Two little rows of red lights illuminated her lenses like a landing strip, and she stepped forward tentatively.

The moment she did, she disappeared up to her knees. She gasped. 'Not again!' It was the same as the bog, only . . . different, somehow. Colder. Extremely cold. She was being sucked into a perilously icy snowdrift. Remembering how she'd escaped last time, Janey reached quickly for her SuSPInder and threw it, up and out, towards the far wall. It caught, and she breathed a sigh of relief as she pulled it taut to trigger the winching mechanism. But nothing happened. It was frozen solid. 'Come on!' she muttered. She tried again, twitching the cable harder, but it was so rigid that Janey was afraid the hook would come loose and she wouldn't be able to get it on top of the wall again.

By now the snowdrift had enveloped her almost to her chest. With no time to try anything else, Janey jammed the frozen end of the SuSPInder into the ice, where it stuck like a javelin. Then, with both arms over her head, she reached for the wire and pulled. It took several attempts to drag herself from the clutches of the snowdrift, and she quickly realized that if she put her left hand on the wire for too long she would slice her frozen fingers off. They'd be left, scattered like a dropped bag of chips, for her father to find later when they pulled out her frozen corpse. 'Gauntlet,' she hissed, fighting for breath as she slipped the glove off her right hand and looped it over the wire. Holding on to both ends, she hauled herself all the way to the top like a monkey. It was immensely hard work, but suddenly she felt her head touch something solid and realized she'd made it to the top of the wall.

She could afford to stop only for a moment to catch her breath; Janey was pretty sure her time would be poor after having to crawl up the SuSPInder. She dropped down into the next quarter of the dome. It was still overwhelmingly cold, and she couldn't actually see the walls through the glare, but suddenly her ears caught a faint but familiar grinding sound. It was the same as last time – only snowy. The walls were closing in, but this time the ground beneath her feet was not stable enough to spark off the Fleet-feet jump. As quickly as her frozen hands would allow her, Janey dropped her ASPIC to the floor, snapped her feet on to it, then jumped as hard as she could. To her delight, the ASPIC formed a surface against which the Fleet-feet could detonate, and seconds later she was perched on top of the platform of ice that had formed when the four walls closed, her board still attached to her feet.

What came next? thought Janey. She pictured G-Mamma on top of the platform, and remembered that she had more or less surfed her way out of the third quarter last time. Only this time it would be filled with snow. If she leaped, she would be submerged by

73

white powder in an instant. That didn't sound like fun, so instead Janey hesitated at the edge of the icy platform, pulled off a tiny piece of SPInamite and threw it back over her shoulder to the centre of the platform.

There was a dull *thwump* and then a rumbling beneath her feet, and suddenly the frozen edifice on which she was standing shook so that she had to rebalance herself just to stay upright. Great shards of ice and snow were separating from the platform and falling into the third quarter beyond, and in moments the whole structure started to implode, shifting and juddering with deafening cracks and more rumbling. I've started an avalanche! thought Janey, but she was not unhappy about it. That was exactly what she had intended. As a whole segment of the platform broke away and thundered into the nothingness below, Janey launched herself after it. She caught the top of the segment at an angle that almost overturned her, but the ASPIC helped her to right herself and suddenly Janey was snowboarding down a vast icy slope, down, down into the white swirling depths of Challenge 3. Janey found herself grinning crazily, and not just because of the wind-rush forcing her lips outwards. This was amazing! But now she was approaching the bottom of the avalanche of snow and ice. Crouching low like she had seen the skiers do on the Olympics, she headed straight for the upturned ice-curl at the bottom of the steepest part of the slope and held her breath . . .

It worked! The next moment she was flying upwards towards the far wall of the third quarter in a record-breaking ski jump that would have seen Janey travelling for miles, if she'd not had to concentrate on getting up and over the wall. Just before the glistening white of the exit wall loomed up before her, the ASPIC started to slow, but Janey wasn't worried. Confidently, she turned herself at right angles to the wall and allowed the ASPIC to hover mere centimetres from the surface as it whipped up the sheer face. Before Janey knew it, she was over the top and down the other side.

The other side. The frightful, terrifying tumble-tube in which Janey had nearly killed herself. Janey fought back the coarse kernel of fear that rose in her throat and strapped her ASPIC back to her thigh. 'It won't be as bad this time,' she told herself firmly. 'This time you're prepared.'

She wiped snow from her Ultra-gogs to see if the walls had started to bend, but even with clear lenses it was impossible to see what was happening around her. White and black melded into a dizzying maelstrom of flashes, as though she was trapped inside a fizzing television screen. But this time she was ready. The sections of the tube snapped into place with a clunk that made Janey's stomach turn over, but she calmly reached for the Spyroscope that would still the whirling snowstorm around her, allowing her to simply step through it with calm, deliberate strides.

75

The churning of the tube had started, even worse in the total white-out; Janey huffed hard a few times to still her nerves and tried not to fight against the buffeting swing of the tube.

But her left hand was numb with cold. As Janey fumbled for the tiny pocket holding the gadget she shoved at it rather than gripped it, and watched with horror as the minuscule glass ball escaped from her fingers and fell into space, to be whisked away by a flurry of wind and snow and ice chips. Within seconds Janey couldn't even see it through the snow whipping around her in a cyclone. The sick feeling opened up deep in her stomach, and the strange juddering and flickering motion of her eyes warned her that she was in trouble, so she barely even registered that she was forced right to the top of the tube on her side, before dropping like a stone down to the bottom of it, being twisted relentlessly and agonizingly as the blackness between the snowflakes gathered and threatened and then wrapped her head in a thick suffocating blanket as she dropped into a dead faint . . .

She awoke in her bed to find G-Mamma throwing chocolate peanuts in the air and catching them in her mouth. 'Oh, you're with us again.' The SPI:KE rattled the box. 'I think there are a few left. Alfie brought them for you.'

'Where is everybody? Why am I in bed?' Janey touched her head gingerly; it was wrapped in an enormous bandage with her Blonde ponytail sticking out of the top. 'I must look like a pineapple.'

'Even patients can be pretty,' said G-Mamma testily. The bandaging was clearly her own work of art. 'You're here because you fainted in the terror-tube, again, and smacked your head on the floor.'

The image of the demonic swirling slowly filled Janey's head and she sighed. 'It just overwhelms me. I thought I'd crack it this time, but I lost the Spyroscope. Did everyone else get through?'

G-Mamma nodded. 'Baby Halo got behind the tube and acid-sprayed the turning mechanism so it didn't work, and Blackbird was so quick behind him that it hadn't started moving again. But anyway, you can ask them yourself in a moment. I was instructed to take you straight to the briefing room as soon as your spying eyes were open. Which they are now, just about.'

Janey still felt woozy as she struggled to her feet. G-Mamma grabbed her arm. 'Come on, speed it up. Let's do one of those army marches: "I don't know but I've been told (five, six, seven, eight), Jane Blonde hates the freezing cold (five, six, seven, eight)!'

'I'm fine, G-Mamma,' said Janey quickly, before she was frogmarched across the campsite shouting G-Mamma raps. She broke into a jog and trotted, a little unsteadily, to the briefing room, with her SPI:KE rollerblading beside her.

They entered the room to find everyone assembled, sitting uneasily on their hard white seats. Alfie and Mrs Halliday looked up and smiled as Janey opened the door, and pointed to the empty chairs next to them. Tish gave her half a grin, which looked more like a smirk. Everyone else's eyes were fixed on the front of the room.

They were looking at her father.

'OK, Janey?'

She nodded. 'I'm fine. Sorry about the whole fainting thing.'

Abe nodded back, a worried smile on his face, and then turned to the group. 'You've all done incredibly well. It's the very end of SPIcamp, and your additional training. I wish I could say that it has all been for fun, but it hasn't. Now the real work starts in earnest.' He paused and sighed before looking levelly at his audience. 'A third member of my support team has been murdered. I need a crack unit to set off immediately to help me discover what's going on and, more importantly, how to stop it. We're going to Antarctica.'

Janey sat up a little straighter in her chair. From the rustling around her, it seemed that everyone else was doing the same. To her joy, the spy instincts that fizzled with anticipation whenever a mission was about to begin were tickling the inside of her ribs. She could even see how it all fitted together: the penguin photo, the glass that turned out to be ice, the snowy final challenge. She gazed back at her father, tingling with pride and excitement.

'I've chosen the unit based on suitability for the particular location and on individual and team strengths,' continued Abe. 'Those of you who are not chosen – it is not an indication of inferiority. You are all very fine Spylets and spies, and you will all be called on to help me in some way very soon.'

Janey sat on her hands to stop them fidgeting. Her nerves jangled.

'So my Spylet team is . . .' Everyone in the room held their breath. 'Al Halo.'

Yes! Janey would get to work with Alfie again. They were a great team.

'Rook,' said Abe, nodding at the slight boy in his black feathered SPIsuit.

Two boys. That would be good, thought Janey.

Abe looked down at his hands again and drew in a deep breath. 'And the final member of the unit . . . Titian Ambition.'

Janey stared, and beside her she heard G-Mamma squeak. She was so convinced that she had heard her father incorrectly that she only just managed to stop herself grinning triumphantly at Alfie. Titian Ambition? Tish was going on this mission instead of her . . . instead of Jane Blonde . . . instead of the daughter of the head of SPI? She couldn't believe it. There must have been a mistake.

But there was no mistake. A map had sprung up on the wall of the briefing room, and Abe was pointing to the location they would be heading for. Without her.

And she knew exactly why.

It was the tumbling tube of terror. Twice now she had fainted inside it. Once she had almost killed herself, and on the other occasion she had flunked the mission entirely. She couldn't withstand those conditions, and there would probably be many occasions when she would have to face them if she went on this mission . . . to Antarctica.

The biggest and most exciting mission of all.

And Jane Blonde would be missing it.

8 blonde to the rescue

Janey had never felt so hurt.

'You do understand why I couldn't choose you, don't you, Janey?' her father had asked gently after the meeting.

'Because you don't want to have a favourite?' Janey knew she wasn't being fair to her dad and that her bottom lip was sticking out, but somehow she couldn't help herself.

'You know I have a favourite.' Abe sighed. 'It's precisely because you're my favourite that I don't want you to take the risk. You would clearly have some difficulty with snowstorms – that's what the tube emulates. And they are rather a frequent occurrence in the Antarctic.'

'I know,' said Janey in a very small voice. 'I just wanted . . .'

'To help. I know. But believe me,' said Abe, 'you'll be a lot more help to me alive.'

He gave her an enormous hug, patted her on the back a few times and said goodbye. Janey watched forlornly as his tall frame loped off into the distance. Who could tell when she'd see him again? And yet Alfie, Rook and Titian Ambition were leaving the very next morning for Antarctica, along with their SPI:KEs, and would get to see him all the time, maybe for weeks and weeks. Blackbird looked equally glum, and she snarled nastily at Rook as he and Tish high-fived. It just wasn't fair.

Alfie didn't seem to think it was fair either, or at least he had trouble looking Janey in the eye when she climbed into the passenger seat of the people carrier on Sunday morning, next to G-Mamma. Mrs Halliday handed Janey an envelope.

'This is for your mum, explaining how the camp went and that I will be recommending you for the scholarship for Everdene. I'm sure she'll be thrilled.'

That will be one parent who's pleased with me, thought Janey grumpily. She stared at Alfie. 'Have fun then,' she said.

'It's not a flipping holiday,' he retorted. 'I'll probably come back dead and frozen.'

'Great Solly lollies!' G-Mamma tooted on the horn. Janey fastened her seat belt carefully. 'Will you two stop feeling so sorry for yourselves? You, Baby Halo, are off on an icy SPIcy mission, and you're . . . um . . . going home to Mumsy, Blonde. Both sound pretty good to me.'

She was obviously lying. G-Mamma couldn't stand what her old friend Gina Bellarina had turned into now that her spying days were behind her, and there was no way she would have thought going home was on a par with setting off on a mission. For the first time Janey understood how difficult this was for all of them, and she took pity on Alfie.

'You'll be great,' she said to him. 'Just watch that acid spray doesn't get anywhere near my dad.'

'Deal.' Alfie gave her a small smile and slammed the door shut.

Then they were off, careering through the field, with G-Mamma pointing the car gleefully at the horse-SPIRIT. 'OK, gee-gee. Watch your bum, cos here we come!'

'Yuck.'

Janey closed her eyes as the horse's tail loomed ever closer. The car nosed its way through the rounded bottom of the hologram, stuck for a moment and then squirted through the WUSS and out into the cloudy grey of the non-spy world. That's how things seemed all the time in the real world, thought Janey. Colourless. Grey. Boring. She wriggled down in the seat and dozed fitfully with Trouble on her knee, trying not to think about what Rook, Tish and Alfie would be up to right now.

'Home, sweet home,' carolled G-Mamma a couple of hours later as she turned into their street. She

83

ducked down out of sight as the people carrier pulled up outside Janey's house, and pressed a button on her SPI-Pod as Janey jumped out. When the front door opened, Janey heard Mrs Halliday's voice shout, 'Say thank you to your mother for me,' and Alfie's rather less polite, 'If you're not in school tomorrow, you're dead!' Then a small silver suitcase bounced towards her down the path and the car screeched away.

'Bye,' she shouted as her mum appeared in the doorway. She felt rather silly waving at some recorded voices and a hidden SPI:KE, but at least her mum thought that everything was normal. 'Hi, Mum.'

'Sweetheart, you're back earlier than I expected. Thank goodness!' Jean Brown held her daughter tight, then drew her inside. 'The house has been very quiet without you.'

Janey smiled. It *was* nice to be home, even if she wasn't on an exciting mission. 'I've got a letter for you from Mrs Halli . . .' Suddenly she stopped. There were noises coming from the kitchen. 'What's that?'

Jean Brown looked decidedly shifty. 'Oh, I had to cancel lunch with Joy last week, so we thought we'd try again today.'

Joy popped her head around the door. 'Hi, Janey,' she called. 'Cheese and biscuits?'

'No, thanks. I'm not hungry,' said Janey rather crossly. The tornado hadn't put an end to her mother's dating campaign then. That was even more evident when Joy trotted out of the kitchen with a tray of food and the newspaper, with a neat circle around an advert:

SINGLE?
LOOKING FOR LOVE?
COME AND MEET POTENTIAL PARTNERS
AT OUR SPEED-DATING SESSION
25 May,
9 P.M. TILL LATE.

Joy smiled at Janey as the women settled down in the lounge. 'So how are you, Janey? Your mum tells me you're being hothoused for Everdene. My boys are off to Tauntley. What other schools are you thinking of?'

Janey fished in her pocket and handed her mother an envelope. 'I don't need to think about others. Mrs Halliday says I'll definitely get into Everdene.'

'Oh, Janey, that's marvellous!' Jean put down her cracker with Camembert to pat Janey on the knee. 'That school camp was really worthwhile, wasn't it?'

Smashing, thought Janey. No mission for me, and a new-boyfriend plan for you. Great. This was not exactly the homecoming she'd imagined. 'I think I'll go up to my room. Maybe . . . unpack or something.'

Joy looked pointedly at her watch and then said, 'Mind if we catch the one o'clock news, Jean? I like to know what's going on in the world.' She grabbed the remote control and pointed it at the TV, while Janey wondered who could possibly be interested in someone so bossy and boring. Her mum was going to look great next to Joy. Which was not good.

Janey stood up and brushed past her mum, but just as Jean caught hold of her hand as if to apologize for the intrusion, Joy said, 'Well, will you look at that? It's that global warming, I bet.'

'*The iceberg is thought to have originated off the Alaskan coast. What it's doing in a lake in Scotland, nobody is quite sure. Geologists believe it has broken off a bigger iceberg out to sea and has somehow floated down the inlet to the lake.*' The newscaster gave a cheesy grin. '*But there are some who are very happy about it, namely the seal colony who have adopted the iceberg as their new home.*'

As the newscaster turned, shuffling his papers and chatting with his co-presenter, the picture flicked to a large, complacent seal, sunning itself on a silvery slope of ice, and then panned out to show the iceberg in its entirety, poking out of a vast Scottish lake. Tiny in one corner of the screen was an odd building – a very tall structure balanced on a slender pole, for all the world like an enormous lollipop.

'Sol's Lols,' said Janey under her breath.

'Sol's Lols, did you say, Janey? Is that your uncle's factory?' Jean turned back to the television but the programme had changed.

Janey was sure that it was, but she wasn't about to

say so. 'No . . . I mean, how would I know? I've never seen it!'

'Good point,' said her mum.

Now she had to get upstairs, and fast. 'I'm going to unpack,' she said hurriedly, then shot out of the lounge and up the stairs. Once in her bedroom, she ASPIC'ed through to the Spylab next door.

'Check the news for icebergs!' she yelled to G-Mamma, who was having a lie-down on one of her workbenches, with a slice of cucumber over each eye.

'Icebergs, spicebergs,' muttered G-Mamma, levering herself up. 'What are you on about?'

Janey told her about the news item. 'I'm sure it was really near the Sol's Lols headquarters.'

They checked again by Googling the news item, and sure enough, when G-Mamma magnified the picture a hundred times on to the fridge, the lolly structure of the headquarters building could clearly be seen. 'There's something going on,' said Janey. 'A big chunk of ice just pops out of nowhere, really near a SPI location?'

G-Mamma pointed at the fat seal enjoying his siesta on the iceberg.

'Seems fishy to you, does it?' G-Mamma snorted. 'Get it? Fishy? Seals eat fish . . . oh, never mind. Maybe it is a bit suspect.'

'A bit? Copernicus has broken his spies out of captivity in the Antarctic, and that's right where Dad is, and suddenly there's an iceberg at his headquarters?' Janey pulled a Back-boat out of one of G-Mamma's many cupboards. Last time she'd gone to Sol's Lols HQ it had been very useful. 'They know there's nobody covering Sol's Lols.'

She ran around the room, yanking open cupboard doors and pulling out hats and scarves, a new Girl-gauntlet and a woolly left glove, and a broader ASPIC she'd spotted on a back shelf, white and gleaming and decorated with pink snowflakes. 'Is this a snowboard?'

G-Mamma was watching her with folded arms. 'Kinda. It's an ice pick.'

'Oh.' Janey looked at the board, disappointed. 'But aren't ice picks supposed to have pointy bits on them?'

'Not an *ice pick*,' said G-Mamma. 'An ISPIC: Ice SPI Conveyor. It'll get you around in snowy conditions much better than your ASPIC, which can freeze up after too long in the cold.'

'Great!' Janey added it to the pile on the workbench. 'Then I think I'm ready to go.' She wrapped a fluffy scarf around her neck, jammed on some pink fluffy earmuffs and grinned at her SPI:KE.

'You're going nowhere, Missy Christmas! Better go and spend some QT with that mother of yours or she might get suspicious.'

Janey stopped short. G-Mamma was right. Not only would her mum wonder what had happened to her if she disappeared now, but the news teams sent to cover the iceberg might question what a young girl in a Lycra snowsuit was doing crawling all over it in the middle of the afternoon. 'OK, but I'm going tonight,' she said eventually.

'Yes, you are.' G-Mamma suddenly grinned delightedly. 'Seems like you're getting your icy mission after all, Blondette. Cold and bold, that's you, girly-girl. Cold and bold!'

The rapping had begun before Janey could get out of the room.

> *'Yo, there's a story to be told*
> *About a Spylet cold and bold.*
> *Cold and bold, yeah, good as gold!*
> *Cold and bold and not too old!*
> *Yerp-yerp, let me hear you,*
> *Yerp-yerp!'*

Back home, Janey tried not to laugh on her way downstairs. Her dad might think that he didn't need her, and that she couldn't cope in snowy conditions, but here was her chance to prove him wrong. She was going to help him whether he liked it or not.

Jane Blonde was back in action.

icebergs, spicebergs

As Janey's cells shot out into the stratosphere, thinking became a little more difficult, but she still had enough power in her separated brain particles to hope that they'd got the footprint right. If the Satispy by which she was now whizzing around the Earth didn't land her in the correct place – directly on top of the iceberg – then she was in for a cold, damp night. She'd left a pillow in her bed to look like her, but she'd better be back in time to dry out.

She tried to focus on the downward journey as her various body parts began to drift back together and one eyeball and then the other returned to their rightful positions. Her nose took another moment to arrive, just as her feet reconnected with her ankles. Below her was the iceberg, and there, visible through the night-vision lenses of her Ultra-gogs, was the plump, lazy seal as seen on TV.

'Whoops!' said Janey. She didn't have an awful lot

of control over where she landed, but she knew that seals could be quite nasty and territorial; she certainly didn't want to make one mad by falling on it, so she angled her legs to the left and managed, just, to avoid contact by landing at an awkward angle and slithering over the side of the iceberg. Just before she plummeted into the freezing water, Janey plunged her frozen ponytail into the ice. Like a tiny platinum axe, it split the solid iceberg just enough to wedge itself into a crack enough to stop Janey's slide into the water. She ground to a cold and painful halt, her feet dangling perilously over the icy depths.

'Not as painful as a seal bite,' she told herself sternly, then stopped short. As her Ultra-gogs had kicked in only when she was just above the seal, she had no information yet to tell her whether there was anything – or anyone – but seals on the little frozen mountain. For all she knew, the other side of the iceberg could be swarming with spies. Added to that was the fact that various spies involved with her past missions had been turned into animals by her father's processes, so the seals themselves might be the enemy. Anchoring herself on her bottom, Janey slid upwards until her hair popped out of its crevice, and looked around.

The lazy seal peered at her with eyes like chocolate buttons, and for one moment Janey was very tempted to reach over and pat it. How could something so cute be dangerous? Then she checked herself.

Trouble was about as adorable as an animal could get, but if he didn't like or trust someone then he made them very aware of the fact, spitting and arching his back and sometimes popping out his lethal sabre claw. At least this seal appeared to be on its own.

On hands and knees, Janey crawled around the entire iceberg. It was the size of a large house or maybe the roof of a small palace, with its craggy outline and slippery sloping surfaces. It took her about twenty minutes to go full circle, during which time she met a dozen more seals tucked away in sheltered corners, found a series of little holes that she'd seen on the TV (where geologists had bored down to discover more about the iceberg) and negotiated a lot of chilly, jagged ice.

'G-Mamma,' she said into her SPIV – the SPI Visualator she hung around her neck whenever she was on a mission, 'I can't see anything funny about this iceberg. Other than that it's here where it shouldn't be.'

G-Mamma's mouth appeared, chewing furiously.

'What are you eating?' hissed Janey.

'Cake,' mumbled G-Mamma. 'Battenberg. You know, iceberg, spiceberg, Battenberg – it was driving me wild. So is it time for the Back-boat?' she said indistinctly through a mouthful of marzipan.

Janey nodded. 'I'll get to the shore and go up to Sol's Lols, see what's going on up there.'

'Check in again when you get there.' An enormous

upright thumb appeared in the SPIV, and then it fell silent.

Grinning, Janey reached around for her Back-boat. It looked exactly like an ordinary school backpack, but as soon as she flung it in the water it let out an enormous hiss, startling a couple of the seals. They slid into the water, alarmed, as the little rectangle of rubber expanded, inflated and turned into a decent-size dinghy with a small but powerful outboard motor. Janey climbed in a little unsteadily, keen to stay out of the water herself, and pretty soon she was safely installed. She pulled the cord to start the motor and puttered across to the lake's edge.

Beyond the bundles of reeds she could see the tall lolly of Sol's Lols, mostly in darkness now as it was the middle of the night. It was all Janey could do not to laugh – the only other time she had been here was for her very first mission, when she had known so little it was amazing she hadn't been killed. Now here she was, alone, unworried, trusting that all her spy instincts that sat below the surface would ensure that she would triumph.

Janey drew up at a small pebble beach and looked around. Nothing. She was relieved to find there were no reporters camped out nearby, but when she climbed to the top of the small shale hillock that cut off the lake from the grounds of Sols Lols she discovered that there was nothing else either. 'Zoom, illuminate,' she instructed her Ultra-gogs. Now, through the enhanced binocular vision of her spy-glasses, she could look around the whole of the building. It sat in darkness. Apart from a lone security guard, who appeared to be playing *Grand Theft Auto* and not doing much security, Sol's Lols was empty.

'Oh.' Janey was almost disappointed. She'd been so sure that she'd get here to find hordes of enemies poisoning the place with their evil, and she'd been even more sure that she'd be able to take them on single-handed and win back her father's favour. In truth, she'd been looking forward to the battle. 'Maybe I'm turning into G-Mamma,' she thought. 'G-Mamma,' she said into the SPIV, 'there's nothing here. My spy instincts must be out of tune . . . I might as well— Hang on.'

'Have you seen something?' squeaked her SPI:KE, as excited as Janey at the thought of a proper mission.

'No, but I've just had an idea while I was thinking about my instincts. Which are all under the surface, aren't they?'

In the Visualator screen G-Mamma's round eyes blinked rapidly. 'You've lost me.'

'What's special about icebergs?'

'I don't know! They're . . . pointy? Slippy? They . . . star in films with Leonardo wotsisname?'

'Yes!' hissed Janey. 'Ships like the *Titanic* bump into them because most of an iceberg is UNDER THE SURFACE.'

'Aha!' G-Mamma's face started to bop up and down as she started one of her cheerleading chants. 'She's got it, oh yeah; Spylet's got it, oh yeah! Hey, where are you . . . ?'

Without waiting for instructions, Janey had turned around, jumped back into the boat and pushed herself out on to the lake. As soon as the Back-boat was in deeper waters, she chewed hard on her SPIder and tipped herself over the edge. The water was icy, and in seconds she could feel every bit of her that wasn't protected by her SPIsuit start to pucker with cold. Her cheeks ached with it as oxygen shot through her nasal and throat passages, but she tried to ignore it as she forced herself deeper into the black depths, moving towards the iceberg. Treading water, she strained to see through the Ultra-gogs. What could she make out? A light . . . a light of some kind, and shapes moving around in it, but nothing she could work out. It was too cold and too dark to be clear.

She broke the surface, gasping. 'G-M . . . M . . . Mamma . . . There's something g . . . going on . . . but I can't stay in the water.'

'Climb back in the boat, Blonde,' instructed G-Mamma, 'and X-ray the iceberg.'

Once in the boat, Janey pointed her face at the iceberg and muttered an instruction to her Ultra-gogs. The ray first revealed a dozen or so seal skeletons, just as they would appear on a hospital X-ray.

95

Below the surface of the water it was hard to make anything out, but Janey did notice a large outline, just below the waterline. It was seal-shaped, but it wasn't throwing out a skeleton like all the other seals.

'Okey-doke, Blondey, get closer and hold the Gogs up to the SPIV,' instructed G-Mamma.

Janey edged the Back-boat as close as she could to the iceberg. In the water beneath her loomed the dark outline of yet another sleek, enormous seal, and Janey clung to the sides of the dinghy as the seal's movements rocked it from side to side. 'I'm X-raying now,' she said as the turbulence subsided. 'Um, take a picture.' To Janey's relief, her glasses clicked and whirred. She held the SPIV up to the Ultra-gogs. 'Can you see that?'

'Whoo, I certainly can!' G-Mamma clapped her hands ecstatically. 'And it's not a real-deal genuine seal at all. I've never seen one before, but I've heard about them. Can you see that little wheel inside it? And the other mechanisms? It's a mini-submarine disguised as an aquatic mammal, used only by spies, as far as I know – a Navy Seal. Get in there, Blonde!'

Janey looked around as she heard G-Mamma clapping and chanting,

'We've got a seal,
A seal with a wheel,
And how does that feel?
It's a Navy Seal!'

Janey grinned. Here was a new challenge. The mini-sub was completely submerged, and she couldn't begin to imagine how she was supposed to get into it without the right code or control. There was certainly no way, however, that she was going to find out by hanging around on the surface of the water. Grabbing her SPIder again, she backward-rolled over the edge of the boat and swam down to the Seal.

Adjusting her Ultra-gogs, Janey paddled all around the submarine, which didn't take long – although it was vast for a seal (and looked amazingly like one), it was tiny for a submarine. Janey estimated that it would hold one person, who would have to get in at the back and lie full length inside the Seal.

Swimming as quickly as she could, Janey made her way to the triangular fin that pointed out from the back of the mini-sub. Below it were two large feet, or . . . propellers! Looking at them more closely, Janey could see that these flippers would waggle back and forth to drive the mini-sub through the water. The entrance had to be somewhere around the tail fin. There! thought Janey, spotting a ring around the body of the Seal, a few inches up from the tail. The tail fin was actually a seal-sized plug that screwed in like the top of a hot-water bottle.

Janey beached the Navy Seal up on the iceberg, so that it was half in, half out of the water, and scrambled up beside it. Once its tail was clear of the lake, she took hold of the fin and pulled. Nothing. She tried to brace her feet against the surface of the iceberg, but couldn't get any grip and instead found herself slipping down and under the submarine. It was too close; any more mishaps and she might just find herself trapped between the Seal and the iceberg, never to be released.

Suddenly she heard a noise below her. Two more Navy Seal subs were about to emerge from the cloudy depths of the lake. Janey couldn't hang around any longer. She needed to be either inside the Navy Seal, or out of the way completely. So she turned to the trusty gadget that had saved her dozens of times before.

'I wish Trouble was here,' she muttered, thinking enviously of his sabre claw. With mere seconds to go before she was discovered, she held up her Girl-gauntlet and popped out her new titanium blade from the index finger. Wriggling it into position in the ring around the tail-end of the Navy Seal, she started to saw. Just as the noses of the other two Seals peeked above the surface, Janey felt the tail give under the pressure of her Girl-gauntlet; she chiselled away for a moment more, then grasped the tail in her Gauntleted hand and twisted. 'Yes!' She'd probably broken the screw mechanism – it might even leak – but at least she could get out of sight.

The plug-end of the submarine now lay on the iceberg behind the body of the Seal, and there would be nobody to fasten it up again after she crawled inside. Quickly Janey squatted down and thrust her entire body into the Navy Seal. Next she positioned her Fleet-feet facing the plug-end of the submarine. 'Don't let me down,' she said under her breath. Her Fleet-feet had worked magnetically before, and to her delight this time was no exception. The metal tail of the Navy Seal spun on the ice a couple of times then headed straight for her Fleet-feet and the plug slammed into place. She was locked inside the Seal. Janey whooped loudly, then reached out her hands for the controls.

'Where . . . where? What do I need? Oh, it must be that,' Janey muttered.

There were two buttons in front of her – a red one marked 'Launch Missile' and a green one labelled 'Go' – as well as a joystick. She smacked the green button and ducked her head as two Navy Seals glided past her, straight into the side of the iceberg. Then she made her way down into the chill, inky depths of the water, towards a mysterious light in the distance and the other two Navy Seals, who appeared to be burrowing straight into the rocky sides of the lake.

sol's lols
revisited

'G-Mamma, this is wrong,' said Janey.

A booming voice erupted from her chest. 'What's wrong? Don't get yourself trapped in there, Bungling Blondey. I'm not right behind you this time.'

Janey winced. She didn't want to remember the terror-tube incidents. 'I'm looking at something very peculiar. Right under the lake, just round from this little shale beach I was on, the cliff goes way down. And there's a hole in it with light coming out of it.'

'You mean the cliff's going to collapse? Get yourself out of there, Blonde, and that's an order!' G-Mamma's voice was shrill with worry.

'It's not going to collapse – at least I hope not, because there are loads of Navy Seals, and . . . divers, yes, ordinary divers, going in and out of the hole. And I just saw two Seals disappear straight into the iceberg. There must be tunnels, in the cliff and in the iceberg.'

'Which means it's not an iceberg at all, it's

a spiceberg! Some offshore spy station. The only question is, is it your father's?'

Janey had no idea. Just because her father was involved in a mission at the Antarctic didn't mean he would have stopped operations elsewhere. There was every chance that these were her father's spies. But what would they be doing under the lake? There was only one way to find out. 'I'm going through the hole,' she said firmly.

G-Mamma sounded as though she was smiling. 'Go to it, Blondette.'

So to it she went, right up to the cliff-face, nudging her way along between other Navy Seals. She couldn't see in to assess whether the Seal pilots looked like friend or foe – one-way glass, she suspected – but just to be sure she couldn't be recognized, she tucked her ponytail down the back of her SPIsuit and thrust her red woolly hat over the top.

'Here we go,' she murmured. The massive hole in the cliff-side was only a few metres away. Keeping her face as much out of sight as possible, Janey pushed the little wheel in the Seal slightly upwards and entered the tunnel.

'Wow!' she gasped. It was not at all like Janey had imagined it would be, like pot-holing, having to squeeze herself along a tube like a rat in a drainpipe. This tunnel resembled an underwater motorway, with heavy traffic of Seals, slightly bigger submarines with great drills on the front of them that reminded Janey of swordfish, and occasional lone divers swimming in either direction in strict lanes.

The tunnel was gradually narrowing, and Janey quickly worked out why there was so much traffic. The drill-fronted mini-subs were widening the neck of the tunnel and the Navy Seals moved the rubble away. Which just left the divers. As another lone frogman passed her on his way along the tunnel, Janey realized instantly what she had to do.

'Nice knowing you, Navy Seal,' she told her mini-sub. She'd actually become quite used to manoeuvring through the water in what felt like a big metal sleeping bag, but she knew now that the machine was too big for the next stage of her journey. Blonde wriggled her feet against the stopper at the tail end of the Seal, popped her SPIder into her mouth and pushed her hands backwards off the steering wheel so that she drifted gently backwards into the water. Let's hope it's not too far, she thought, a little anxiously – her SPIsuit was fine for normal water conditions, but was no match for the dense protection of a wetsuit in the chilly water.

Using her Ultra-gogs for guidance, Janey swam forward to where she had seen the diver disappear. It was just as she'd thought. A drill-fronted mini-sub had forged a hole through the cliff-side, but it was only wide enough at this point to take a man, or, in this case, a Spylet. Janey hesitated for a moment, treading water. If she was confronted in here, she would be completely stuck. Of course, she could be among friends, but . . .

If she was among enemy spies, she could be in grave danger. On the other hand, if she survived, she'd show all the team in Antarctica that she was worthy of her Spylet status – that she was, in fact, truly sensational. Gripping the edge of the narrow tunnel with her hands, Janey launched herself forward and kicked her feet furiously.

The water around her became more turbulent. Someone was coming up behind her. Janey waggled her feet harder but when she glanced back through the water she spotted a black dot, increasing in size – it was a diver's helmet, getting ever closer.

The tunnel now seemed to be heading upwards. Moments later Janey realized her body was almost vertical, and suddenly beside her there were metal rungs. It was a little underwater ladder. The head and shoulders of her pursuer were now quite visible. Time for a bit of help. Grabbing hold of one of the rails above her head, Janey slammed her feet against the bottom rung. Her Fleet-feet exploded, sending her hurtling through the water so fast that her hat slid off her head, until she was launched several metres into the air like water from a whale's spout.

From her vantage point as she flew through the air, Janey's brain quickly computed several things.

One, if she angled her body slightly, she could land on the poolside instead of back in the water. Two, there would be a very surprised diver following her out very soon, and she needed to get out of his way, as well as out of the reach of the three burly men with clipboards who were staring at her slack-jawed as she sailed over their heads. And three, she had been here before, on her first mission as Jane Blonde.

'So no trace of the metal . . .' The startled voice of one of the men trailed off as Janey tumbled over in mid-air and angled herself towards the floor.

It was all very familiar – she was in a swimming-pool room. Sol's swimming-pool room. The tunnel led straight into it, right into the heart of Sol's Lols. She had been trapped in here before by the Sinerlesse, and as she connected with the tiled floor surrounding the pool Janey sensed that she was probably in every bit as much danger as she had been that night.

'Oi!' gargled an outraged voice. It was the diver, thrashing furiously in the middle of the pool. 'What sort of stupid trick was that? You could have given me the bends!'

'Sorry,' said Janey, backing towards the wall as a large man with a beard and a clipboard stalked towards her. 'Had a bit of a . . . malfunction.'

'What department are you?' barked one of the men with clipboards.

'Um, surveillance,' said Janey, nodding sternly as if

to show they were all in this together. She even pointed at a strange black mark on the edge of the pool, to show how seriously she took her job. In fact, now she'd spotted it, she would have liked to get a closer look. Something about it was oddly familiar.

Her ploy didn't work. 'Very funny,' said the man. 'We're all surveillance, aren't we? Kind of what spies do. And I'm not sure we've seen you before. Which division? Geology, aeronautical engineering, assassination . . .'

'Assassination?' squeaked Janey. Wasn't that killing people? She realized it had come out as a question. 'Erm, yes, assassination.'

A second man came up behind the bearded one, brandishing his clipboard. 'That's my department. I thought I'd had all my assassins through already, and I've redirected everyone to Antarctica since there was nobody here to assassinate when we arrived.' Janey breathed a sigh of relief – her father had emptied the place before heading off South – as the man flipped through a couple of pages attached to his board. 'No, nobody left on here. What name is it?'

Janey thought quickly. The third man was approaching too, and the diver had scrambled out of the pool and was making his way over towards the group. 'I'm a spy – I'm not giving you my name!'

The bearded man rolled his eyes. 'Come on, Blondey. We don't have time for this.'

'Yeah, Blondey,' sneered the second man. 'We can always put you on rubble-moving.'

Janey hoped they would never realize how close they had come to the truth. She was trying to stammer something – anything – in reply, when the bearded man cocked his head to one side as though he'd just thought of something. He looked at his colleague. 'Blonde girl. Short. Skinny legs. Silver spysuit. Where've I seen that before?'

And at that moment the diver roared in outrage, 'That's right, it's her, innit? Blonde, Jane Blonde!'

'Oh my life, that's why she's familiar. She's one of the ones we're meant to be assassinating,' said the bearded man, flinging his clipboard to one side. 'The big C will be very happy with me.'

Janey shook her head. 'You won't get me,' she said with more conviction than she felt.

'Yeah? You'll be sorry you said that,' said the diver.

Janey was sorry, very sorry indeed, as four strapping men reached out to seize her. She knew from past experience that it was very difficult to get out of here. The door became invisible when closed, there were no windows, and even the spout in the floor through which she'd entered would be filled with divers, or could even be closed off at the click of a switch for all she knew. She danced backwards, but pretty soon she'd be trapped up against a wall. This time she didn't even have her Back-boat to blast through the ceiling.

She looked around desperately. All four immense figures were closing in on her. 'G-Mamma,' she hissed into her SPIV, even though she knew there was very little her SPI:KE could do. At least she could try to let her know what was going on. 'Enemy spies all over Sol's Lols. No gadgets left with me. And I'm on their list for assassination . . .'

But just as the bearded man's hands moved towards her throat, Janey remembered something she did have with her. Her fingers reached into a pocket on her sleeve and closed around the tiny object in there, the object that Trouble had dropped into her lap when he understood he wasn't coming on this particular mission, and to her relief she felt immediately the rush of wind that threatened to force her fingers apart. It managed instead to send the four men hurtling backwards, hair, beards and faces distorted by the hurricane that blasted them against the walls of the pool room and sent two of them straight into the water. Water crashed up the sides of the room, forced out of the pool by the cyclone battering it from above, and the ceiling, unable to withstand the pressure from within, shattered and sprayed tiny glittering discs of glass everywhere, like money tossed from a fairy's purse. It was almost fun to watch, thought Janey, as she was elevated on her great invisible cushion of air as high as the hole where the ceiling had been. She battled forward to the wind zone at the edge of the Spyroscope's coverage, stepped on to a nearby roof and closed her fist tightly around the gadget. At once the wind dropped and she peeked back through the splintered roof. 'Told you you wouldn't get me,' she called, and she laughed at the four outraged faces below. Then she turned and sprinted along the rooftops, right away from the swimming pool and the people who now knew for definite that she was Jane Blonde, Sensational Spylet.

She wasn't finished though. She still didn't know what they were up to, other than aiming to kill any SPIs they might ever have heard of . . . Once at ground level, Janey turned back on herself and ran below a hedge until she came up to the reception area. 'Zoom,' she said to her spy glasses, taking in as many details as she could, even as she heard shouts behind her. The men were on her trail.

'G-Mamma,' she hissed into her SPIV, 'I'm pretty sure they're Copernicus's men. They're tunnelling under the lake and popping up in the Sol's Lols swimming pool, looking for . . . some metal.' What had that man said? Geology, aeronautical engineering, assassination. It didn't make any sense to Janey – yet. 'And there are these weird marks everywhere,' she continued, spotting another across the floor of reception. 'They remind me of something, something I've seen recently. They're all shiny and black.'

'Shiny and black?' repeated G-Mamma. 'Like that man's wetsuit behind you?'

Janey whipped around and, sure enough, an angry diver was launching himself towards her. 'Satispy!' she yelled.

'Already done,' reported G-Mamma, as Janey started to disintegrate.

But not before Janey wondered again what those dark, viscous marks reminded her of. G-Mamma was right. It was something like a wetsuit. But what?

Jane Blonde intended to find out.

out in the cold

'Couldn't you have got a sample?' moaned G-Mamma back at the Spylab. 'I mean, "black and shiny"? Great groovy gadgets! It's not much to go on, is it?'

'I couldn't get close enough,' said Janey, emerging from the Wower in a long nightdress and a rather fetching pair of fluffy lamb-shaped slippers that Bert had sent from Australia. 'I'd only just spotted it when you Satispied me out of there.'

She'd decoded and debriefed before de-Wowing, so G-Mamma was up to speed with the takeover of Sol's Lols and the apparent search for some kind of metal at the HQ.

'I'll go back tomorrow night,' said Janey, smacking the fireplace on the ten-past-two location that opened the tunnel between the two rooms. 'Right now I need to go to bed in case Mum looks in on me.'

At that G-Mamma slapped a hand to her forehead. 'Yikes, clumsy mumsies! Mean Jean will sack me. Let's get over to your place before she gets home.'

Janey yelped as G-Mamma prodded her in the behind, urging her more quickly through the fireplace tunnel. She'd been in more than enough tight spaces with someone right behind her for one night. 'What are you doing?' She sprang to her feet in her bedroom and helped G-Mamma out of the grate.

'I completely forgot!' G-Mamma wrenched open the door and ploughed down the stairs two at a time. 'I'm supposed to be babysitting.'

'For me?' said Janey, following her SPI:KE into the lounge, where G-Mamma now sat with her feet on the coffee table, attempting to look interested in a complex tapestry of Windsor Castle.

'Who else would I be babysitting for in your house? Of course it's you.' She pricked her finger with the needle and howled furiously. 'That's it! I'll put it through the Wower later – it'll be even better than the Bayeux Tapestry of old Harold with his eye out. Mine will have real blood!'

Bewildered, Janey sat down slowly on the edge of the TV chair, the one her mum liked to sit in when she watched the news or one of her forensic-investigation programmes. 'I don't understand. Mum hates you! She'd never leave me with you. And she was here when I pretended to go to bed a few hours ago.'

'Ah gneeuow,' said G-Mamma indistinctly

as she sucked her pricked finger, just as surprised as Janey. 'But she popped round while you were doing your icy SPIcy stuff in bagpipe-land. Said she'd decided to go somewhere at the last minute, and would I mind just sitting in for a few hours as you were already asleep anyway. I came right over.'

Janey shook her head. 'This isn't right. One, Mum never goes out. Two, she can't stand you. And three, she didn't say who she was going out with. It could have been a horrible trick or . . .' She stopped, suddenly noticing the newspaper on the table. The red-circled advert stood out like a pimple. 'Oh no. She's gone speed-dating with Joy.'

G-Mamma's eyes bulged so much they looked like they might fall out of her head. 'Speed-dating? Your mother?' And then she rolled on the sofa, laughing so hard that her tight orange dress started to strain at the seams. 'Wait till your father hears about that one!'

'There's the door!' Janey leaped out of her seat. 'Go!'

'No, you go,' said G-Mamma sharply. 'For once I'm the one who's meant to be here, not you.'

Janey raced up the stairs and into her room just in time to hear her mother say, 'Night, Joy. Yes, three numbers! I wonder when I'll hear from them,' and then slam the door behind her as she came in.

'I'm back,' Jean called softly to G-Mamma. 'Thanks, Miss . . . errr . . . Mamma.'

'Call me Rosie,' Janey heard G-Mamma say kindly. 'And it was no trouble. Any time. Your little angel is sleeping like the dead. I-I mean, she's fast asleep.'

There was a bit of mumbled conversation and then two front doors banged in quick succession. Janey stayed in bed just long enough to hear the bedroom door creak as her mother popped her head round to check on her. Then she whisked through to the Spylab again. G-Mamma was busy piling things on to the workbench, singing softly:

'Here we go gathering gadgetry,
Gadgetry, gadgetry,
Here we go gathering gadgetry,
On a cold and frosty morning.'

'So what did she say?' demanded Janey.

'She said speed-dating is great fun.' Adding a pair of Roller-blades to the pile in front of her, G-Mamma snorted loudly. 'Even suggested I should try it. Me! As if.'

It didn't sound good. She'd found it fun. And three numbers – that's what her mum had said. Did that mean she was going to be dating three different men? Suddenly Janey noticed properly what G-Mamma was doing. She pointed to the mound of SPI-buys. 'Where are you sending me?'

'Honey-child, can you see yourself in these?'

said G-Mamma, holding up an enormous pair of aqua wellingtons. 'These are for me. "Gumboots" we call them in Oz. I'm off to Dubbo Seven to see Bert.'

Janey stared in disbelief. This was disgusting! Not only was her own mother sneaking out for late-night rendezvous with unknown speed-daters, but now G-Mamma appeared to be zipping off on little romantic expeditions too. 'What about checking the shiny black samples?'

'You haven't got any yet,' G-Mamma pointed out. 'I'll be back in a few days. It's not like I'm going to the other side of the world. Oh, well, OK, it is, but it's fine when you travel by SPIral staircase. SPIV me if you come up with anything. Now, back to bed with you.'

Irritated, Janey slumped against the bench as her SPI:KE stepped into the rotating elevator and shot off through the centre of the Earth. Now she was completely on her own – apart from her mum, who didn't seem to notice whether Janey was around or not at the moment. And she seemed to have completely forgotten about Abe Rownigan, which was rather inconvenient, since he was, although she didn't know it, her husband.

Even Alfie was away. There was nobody to talk to although . . . Janey decided it was time to use an every-day gadget that lots of people, not just spies, carried in their pocket. Tapping into G-Mamma's keyboard, she found the phone-from-your-computer information and keyed in Alfie's mobile number. Suddenly his face bounced up on to the computer screen.

'Alfie, it's me,' Janey said, then kicked herself as she realized that he would be able to see her face on the screen of his mobile.

'So it is,' he said, glancing over his shoulder.

'How's it going?'

'Can't really say.'

He was being a very proper Spylet, much to Janey's annoyance. 'Is everyone OK? How's my dad?'

Alfie looked as though he was chewing the question over. Eventually he said, 'Well, that would be telling, wouldn't it?'

'Is anyone around?' He was being very odd and secretive, which was fine when they were being spies, but not when she'd just called him as a friend.

Alfie glanced left and right. 'Nope.'

'Good. I've got loads to catch up on. Wait till I tell you where I've been tonight . . .'

But Alfie shook his head. 'I'm a bit busy, Janey. I'm sort of in the middle of a table-tennis tournament with Rook – he's a bit down because Blackbird's, um, not here. And your dad was talking about a lunchtime meeting . . .'

Turning back to the computer, Janey toggled through to the Google bar and found the world clock. It was midnight at home, but midday where Alfie was. 'Got it,' she said. 'Why don't you call me later?'

'If I've got time,' said Alfie with a great exaggerated shrug.

'But I'll be—'

Alfie sighed. 'Janey, not now, OK?'

And all at once it looked as though he wasn't giving an excuse to get himself out of trouble. He looked just . . . bored. Fed up with her demanding his attention. Or perhaps even more than that, thought Janey. It was as if he couldn't care less.

Janey cut off the connection without even saying goodbye. What was the point? Nobody had any interest in her any more. Parents? Not interested. Her mother was too busy speed-dating eight strange men with her boring bossy friend, while her father was running around the Antarctic with his hand-picked group of spies, which didn't include his own daughter. Meanwhile her SPI:KE was combing sheep in Australia and 'getting flirty with Berty', as G-Mamma herself might describe it. Janey looked down at the lamb slippers that Bert had sent. 'Oh! He *didn't* send them!' Janey had imagined that they'd been posted to G-Mamma, but suddenly it was clear that her SPI:KE had brought them back in person. By the looks of things, there had been previous SPIral journeys to Dubbo Seven that Janey had known nothing about.

As for her best friend, schoolmate and fellow

Spylet, Alfie Halliday, it seemed as if he considered himself too important these days even to call her when she'd asked him to, when she needed a friend, particularly one who was another Spylet. Maybe he was just having too much fun with a new friend who just happened to be a boy.

Janey made her way back to her bedroom, fighting the horrid, barely-remembered tingling across the bridge of her nose. For the first time since the wonderful day G-Mamma had told her she was a Spylet, Janey wondered what would happen if she just welded the fireplace door shut after she'd passed through it into the blank ordinariness of her own bedroom. Maybe nobody would care. They might not even notice.

Perhaps, thought Janey, it was time to turn in her SPIsuit. There wasn't a single SPI who seemed to consider her a good enough Spylet to work with on a consistent basis, and meanwhile the spying was getting in the way of her protecting the one person who DID still appreciate her: her mum. Her ordinary, ex-SPI-with-no-idea mum. Without SPI training and missions she could concentrate more on her schoolwork, and even go on those weekends away to Rome and Barcelona that her mum wanted so much. Apart from the fact that she'd love to go to these places, Janey had a funny feeling that if *she* didn't accompany her mother, someone else might go along instead.

It pained her to even think it, but the more

Janey considered it, as she did many times through that restless night, the more she reached the same conclusion: it was time to forget Jane Blonde. Maybe now it would be better to be just plain old Janey Brown. It seemed almost unreal even to think it, but it also, somehow, felt right.

woe for worms

Janey woke up feeling strangely peaceful, even though she'd slept so badly that she'd tangled the sheets into a fat ball around her legs. It was the hot, uncomfortable feeling of being trapped in her bedding that awoke her. Why had she tossed and turned so much?

Then she remembered the horrible truth.

She wasn't cutting it as a SPI any more. She didn't even seem to be making the grade as a daughter or a friend. So . . . it was time that Jane Blonde was no more. She needed normal friends and at least one normal parent – particularly if she was off to Everdene, leaving Alfie behind. She was retiring, and Janey would go back to being just Janey from now on.

'No more Blonde,' she said firmly.

The words almost stuck in her throat, but as she said them again, almost like a chant, staring at herself in the mirror that G-Mamma had used to write messages on, she found herself liking the sound of them, convincing herself that losing her Spylet self would be a good thing, that being Brown was much to be preferred. 'No more Blonde! No more Blonde!' she yelled at her reflection, smacking her hand down on the desk.

Her mother's head appeared around the door. 'No more what? Are you all right?'

'Oh! No more . . . um . . . pond,' gabbled Janey as her mother stared at her, perplexed. 'They want to put a, er, pond in the school grounds.'

'Wouldn't that be a nice thing?' said Jean.

Of course it would. 'No,' said Janey a little too loudly. 'Because . . . they'd have to dig up all the insects that live in the grass, and a lot of . . . of worms would lose their homes.'

'Worms?'

Janey nodded. wondering how she got herself into these situations. Losing her Blonde alter ego would certainly mean a lot less lying. 'Yes, worms. They have rights too. Some of us are doing a demonstration at school. "No more pond!"' She smiled weakly.

To her surprise, her mum came over and hugged her. 'Well, I'm very glad you and Alfie are prepared to stand up for what you believe in.'

With tears prickling behind her eyes, Janey said, 'It's not Alfie. It's some other friends.'

'Good for you,' said Jean. 'Well, let me know if I can help you do some placards or whatever.'

Janey nearly burst into tears there and then. How could she not devote herself to looking after her mum, saving her from devious daters? No one else's mum would be prepared to spend her afternoon painting 'Save Our Worms' posters. 'Um, maybe after school then, Mum, let's see . . . I guess I'd better get ready now.' Hopefully she'll forget all about it, thought Janey guiltily.

It felt very odd going into school without Alfie – not just without him, but being the only person in the entire school to know where Alfie actually was, and what he was up to. It felt a bit peculiar, too, to be explaining to the one or two people who asked her that she'd been away at a camp with Alfie, and he'd stayed on to do some extra courses. Benjamin Crawley whispered loudly to Andrew McElroy, 'Swot!' and Janey just smiled to herself and sat down. At one time that would have hurt her terribly, but somehow, knowing how much they *didn't* know made her feel much better. And that was OK, she decided. She'd always have her memories of when she was special. Wouldn't she?

All in all, it hadn't been too bad a day, being plain Janey Brown. She found she was almost swinging her bag, so casual and relaxed did she feel, as she sauntered out of the school gates to wait for her mum's van. Perhaps *not* being a SPI was going to be rather nice . . .

A shrill voice shook her out of her reverie. 'Janey, one moment please!'

It was Mrs Halliday. 'You're back,' said Janey, surprised. 'Is Alfie home too?' she asked hopefully.

Mrs Halliday ducked her head to one side and Janey followed her behind a tree. 'Your father's kept all the Spylets down in Antarctica. But Alfie's feeling quite sick, I think. The conditions are very difficult. I thought I should let you know so you can start to prepare.'

'For what?'

'I suspect Alfie will be pulled out of the operation soon.' Mrs Halliday smiled at Janey, her pointed teeth digging into her lips, which were disturbingly red with little strands of skin hanging off them. The conditions really must be hard in Antarctica. 'Your father will need a replacement.'

'Oh,' said Janey, looking at her shoes, 'I'm pretty sure he wouldn't choose me. And anyway, I wouldn't go even if he did.'

'What? If you're needed on a mission, you go. You're a Spylet, Janey.'

Janey shook her head slowly. 'Not any more.' And she walked away, leaving Mrs Halliday in stunned silence.

The silence didn't last long, however. By the time her mother pulled up in the Clean Jean van, Janey was having an argument with her chest. Out of habit she had draped her SPIV around her neck and hidden it under her jumper; now G-Mamma, whom Mrs Halliday had immediately alerted to the fact that Janey was quitting, was putting up a fight.

'But, Blonde, you breathe Spylet, you sleep Spylet, you ARE a Spylet!' G-Mamma wailed, her mood not improved by being awoken at three in the morning Dubbo Seven time. 'What the sleepy sheepies are you on about?'

'I just think it would be better if I stopped,' Janey hissed into her sweater, trying to avoid the stares of passers-by.

'Well, think again, Blondette. You don't decide when you stop. You've got a job. A career. No, a lifetime's vocation! You can't just switch it off.'

'But,' said Janey, swallowing down a hard lump in her throat, 'I'm no good at it any more – I'm not even getting chosen – and I feel like nobody cares whether I do it or not anyway. You're away. Dad . . . doesn't need me. Mum's going out dating.'

G-Mamma blinked like a lizard. 'I'm coming home. Meet me in the Spylab. Over.'

Janey nodded, then shook her head, then nodded again. It was all so confusing. She'd become so used to having two lives that she didn't quite know what to do with herself. What would happen if she just didn't turn up at the Spylab? She couldn't be sacked – she'd given up spying anyway. Maybe she should ask to be brain-wiped. Then all the memories of her incredible

Spylet moments would vanish into the ether and she really would be plain Janey Brown once more. The thought sent a horrible, cold shiver down her spine.

As Janey and her mum walked in through the front door, Janey felt resolved. 'I will go and see G-Mamma, but only when I'm ready,' she told herself. First of all she was going to taste some normality by having a glass of milk and a biscuit with her mum. Jean was closing the door behind her with a secretive smile on her face.

'Are you going out again?' said Janey.

'Not tonight,' her mother replied, that same mischievous grin playing at the corners of her mouth. 'I thought we might work on these instead. I did them this morning.' From the tall cupboard under the stairs she pulled out a number of large square cards, with the words 'Save our worms!' and 'Worms need homes!' daubed on in fluorescent colours. 'We could stick them on to some of those old fence posts in the back garden. Then you'll really have something to demonstrate with.'

'Mum, you're . . . mad. And brilliant,' said Janey, flipping through the dozen or so posters. What she was going to do with them she had no idea, but her mother was all fired up.

'I'll go and get those posts,' Jean said. 'You get the hammer.'

Janey laughed as she read through the rest of the

placards. As well as the first two, there were 'No to the pond!' in vivid green and 'Earthworms need earth!!' in thick orange writing.

'Earth for worms!' she shouted, waving the placard over her head.

'Never mind worms,' hissed a voice above her head. 'Sol needs Spylets!'

G-Mamma was leaning over the banister, gesturing frantically to Janey, who was clearly meant to drop everything and run through to the Spylab.

Janey stood her ground. 'Well, he doesn't need *me*. And the worms do.' She conveniently didn't mention that she'd made the whole pond debacle up.

'Up here, now!' G-Mamma's face was purple with rage and a slight touch of bewilderment.

'No,' said Janey, standing up. 'I'm going to help Mum in the garden. You'd better get back . . .'

'Blonde, if you . . .'

But Janey had already walked away. She felt strangely powerful. It was the right thing to do, surely? She could enjoy some special time with her mum, distract her from dating, avoid certain death. It all made sense. So she hung around in the garden, pulling out old fencing posts and thwacking the sticking-out nails back into the wood. It was quite relaxing really. Fun, even.

'That'll be enough,' said her mum. 'Go and get the bits of card.'

Janey ambled through to the hall, half-expecting to see G-Mamma bobbing up near the ceiling like a blimp, engorged with rage. The SPI:KE wasn't there, and her bedroom door was firmly closed. Janey flicked idly though the cards again. 'Worms, earth, pond,' she muttered. What was she going to do with all these? She could see herself having to hold a lone demonstration at the school gates, looking like an absolute nutter.

But when she came to the bottom card, Janey gasped aloud.

'"Save our Sol!"?' Why had her mother written that? She looked more closely. Her mother hadn't written it, after all. She might have written 'Save our worms' originally, but someone else had written over the last word, etching a great fat capital S over the letter W, and a broad, sweeping L to cover the last three letters of the word. The new writing was sticky, black and shiny, and attached to the top of the L was something glistening. Janey picked it off carefully between her thumb and index finger. It was a tiny black feather.

Rook. Or Blackbird – Janey wasn't sure which. But those three short words – 'Save our Sol!' – told her a hundred things at once. Her father was in trouble. The Spylet twins could be in difficulties too, needing her help. Most importantly of all, as Janey knew by the emotions roaring in her chest, there was no way she could stop being a Spylet now.

Jane Blonde was needed.

'Mum, I'm just going to get changed before we start nailing,' she yelled quickly.

'Good idea,' a faint voice from the garden returned. So Janey turned on her heel with the poster in her hand and sped up the stairs.

'G-Mamma, I'm sorry,' she said breathlessly as she zoomed from her bedroom into the Spylab.

Her SPI:KE was standing in front of the open refrigerator, fanning her flushed face. 'SPIralling after being in one-hundred-degree heat is really not a good idea,' she said faintly. 'And neither is telling me you're giving up Spyleting!'

'I've changed my mind,' said Janey, holding the placard up in front of her.

'Save our Soul? Who sent you that?'

'Not "Soul",' said Janey. '*Sol.* Save my dad. Someone's been into my house today and changed the message, and I'm guessing from the colour that it must have been Blackbird or Rook. Though Rook's with Alfie in Antarctica.'

G-Mamma's eyes narrowed. 'Black and shiny – well, there's our sample. Now I see. Well, if you're sure you're not going to go all sulky on us again, it would seem you have a job to do.'

'I wasn't sulk . . .' Janey ground to a halt. Maybe she had been sulking just a little. Perhaps Titian Ambition was right – Janey didn't like it when she

wasn't being 'sensational'. 'So where should I go first
– Sol's Lols HQ, to check out all those black marks?
Maybe the twins had been there to protect him.'

But G-Mamma was rustling in a cupboard,
distracted. 'I'm sure I got them out . . . Not that they'd
be right for where you're going, but . . .'

She shook her head and flung open another
cupboard. 'Oh well,' she said as a pile of discarded
SPI-buys grew on the floor beside her. 'Your eSPIdrills
would be too flimsy anyway.'

'You can't find my eSPIdrills?' Janey thought
fondly of the extraordinary shoes with which she'd
bored through the centre of the Earth to Australia not
too long ago. 'Am I going to Dubbo Seven?'

But G-Mamma shook her blonde curls vigorously.
'Not this time, Dudette. Tonight, Jane the Insane, I am
sending you south. To Antarctica.'

And Janey couldn't help herself as an enormous
shiver ran down her neck and then engulfed her
completely. Finally she was on her way.

13 poles and penguins

Later that night, after Janey had spent some time planning the worm demo with her mum, she stepped into the new de luxe Wower in G-Mamma's Spylab. Despite the many, many times that Janey Brown had Wowed into Jane Blonde, she still felt the same thrill of power pulsing through her whenever the Wower worked its magic. Eight jets of transformational droplets surged at her from all directions and strong metal arms cradled her as she was massaged into an invigorated state, like a boxer at the edge of the ring.

Today the transformation was to be particularly spectacular. The conditions that close to the South Pole would be extreme, so Janey needed an extreme SPIsuit . . .

As the sparkling droplets shimmered around her and her hair was tweaked into her trademark high platinum ponytail, Janey found herself cocooned in soft thermal layers and an extra-thick vibrant-pink neoprene bodysuit with fur-trimmed earmuffs and hood, sleeves, boots and Girl-gauntlet (and this time she had a thick angora glove on her left hand too). Her ISPIC was clamped to her thigh and her Ultra-gogs were broader than usual and attached firmly to her upper face like a fur-edged swimming mask; with her hood pulled in tightly, only the very tip of her nose would be sticking out, a victim to the cold.

As she opened the Wower door, G-Mamma attacked her face with a tube of Zinc cream. 'Don't want your nostrils nibbled with frostbite,' she said, rubbing the end of Janey's nose. Janey's face warmed up instantly. 'Keep the tube with you. You might find it useful. It is a SPI-buy, after all.'

Janey smiled, and her grin became even wider when she saw herself in G-Mamma's mirror. 'I look like a yeti.'

'A very sleek yeti.' G-Mamma eyed her appraisingly. 'If I was in that get-up, I'd look like a snowball.'

'Will I still need those eSPIdrills?' It seemed likely if she was going to tunnel her way there, but the thought of arriving head down in metres-deep ice and snow wearing summery sandals was rather worrying.

G-Mamma dropped to her knees, revealing some fetching silk pantaloons under her flowery ruffled skirt. 'Hope not. Let me have a little lookee. Yes, as I thought, the Wower's done a great job on these boots.' Janey's regular white Fleet-feet boots had aquired fluff, several layers of leather and some sturdy laces. 'Remember I said the prototype eSPIdrills were like Doc Martens? Well, you are now wearing the latest model – furry SPILL-Drills. That's SPI Long-Legged Drills to you.'

It all became clear a few minutes later when Janey was standing out in G-Mamma's garden among the strawberry plants with G-Mamma fussing around her feet. 'These boots lace up right to the top, but if you do this –' and she untied the laces and spread them around Janey's feet – 'then you can drill away without getting cold tootsies.'

'I'm off then,' said Janey. She couldn't wait to get going. It was hard to believe that just an hour ago she had been planning to hang up her SPIsuit forever. Right now, she never wanted to be out of it again.

'You're not going without this.' G-Mamma rammed a large plastic helmet over Janey's head. It was edged with soft material that fell down around her feet – her SPIFFInG (SPI Furnace/Fire/Incinerator Gear), designed to stop her melting in the heat of the Earth's core. 'And, of course, this.'

'Twubs!' Janey laughed as Trouble nosed his way under the edge of the SPIFFInG. He had also been Wowed for arctic conditions: a double layer of fur made him look more like a striped furry football than a cat, his golden tail was wrapped in a chunky scarf which appeared to have a picture of Windsor Castle on it, and his feet were encased in four tiny fur boots exactly like Janey's SPILL-Drills. 'You are one cute kitty!'

Trouble purred loudly, then jumped into her arms and snuggled in for the journey. 'All right, my little SPIcicles,' said G-Mamma. 'Let the spin begin!'

The SPI:KE entered the coordinates and pressed the tiny snowflake on the SPILL-Drills, and, just as Janey had done when wearing the eSPIdrills, she began to rotate. They spun slowly around the flower bed, driving her soles into the earth and spraying unpicked strawberries in a jammy mess all over G-Mamma's skirt. 'Sorry, G-Mamma,' said Janey, although it was hard not to laugh when her SPI:KE came back into view, scooping the strawberry pulp off herself and eagerly eating it.

Janey and Trouble speeded up. Soon G-Mamma was just a blur, and then only her pantaloons and feet were visible, and soon all Janey could see around her was earth, worms and the roots of plants. As their spinning increased to a mighty whirr, the Spylet and Spycat plunged further into the ground.

Soon they were drilling through water, then magma, then they slowed as they reached the solid metallic core of the Earth. Whatever it was made of was so resilient – almost impenetrable – that the first time Janey had travelled this way she had stopped short and thought she would probably die in an unthinkably hot, bone-crushingly pressured, unbelievably deeply buried coffin.

This time they slowed again. Trouble pushed his nose nervously into the crook of Janey's arm as they ground to a halt. With a little prayer to her SPILL-Drills Janey jumped. Success! There was a small explosion which sparked the drills into life again, and they were off, on through the steely Earth's core, out into lava and molten rock, further on until they were spinning through dense black rock and a layer of ice many times the height of Janey. Suddenly Janey felt her feet waggling around in the open air and she let out a muffled shout of joy; she might be upside down, but at least she'd made it! She pushed herself feet first out of the hole, and at last she and Trouble scrambled out into the chill and dark of Antarctica. She was in the land of the South Pole. Near her dad and the other Spylets.

'Come on, Twubs,' said Janey, giving her cat's head a rub. In spite of his husky-thick fur, he was shivering so much that the scarf around his tail was working its way off and on to the ice. Janey tugged it down again and attempted to look around. A vicious wind billowed around them; standing up, Janey had to lean straight into it to make any headway at all. Not that she knew where to go. It seemed that she had made it to Antarctica, but where exactly were they supposed to go? 'G-Mamma will know,' she told herself, but in these temperatures she was reluctant to unzip her SPIsuit to extract her SPIV.

To her delight, however, someone seemed

133

to know exactly where to go. Trouble staggered purposefully through the billowing wind, wobbling this way and that but refusing to be knocked off course. Janey bent over to grab his tail, and bit by bit the two of them shuffled along in the semi-darkness.

'I hope you know what you're doing, Twubs,' bellowed Janey, as he ploughed on determinedly. 'How big is Antarctica anyway? How are we going to find my dad in this?' It was difficult to see further than Trouble's nose in the grey half-light and the flurries of snow. The packed ice beneath their feet made the going very slippy, and Janey was jealous of Trouble's claws as she slithered along in his wake.

Just then Janey felt Trouble's tail stiffen, and the next moment he was bounding along, skittering on the ice, towards a shadowy figure that had appeared nearby. Janey grabbed her SPI-Pod quickly. Just below one of the dials was the word 'MIC'. Spinning the dial to ten, Janey raised the SPI-Pod to her lips and yelled, 'Hey! Wait for me!'

In any normal environment the noise would have been deafening, but here in the Antarctic her amplified voice still made very little impression above the wind. The figure waved; Janey peered at it and staggered forward, and suddenly found herself staring up at the surprised, pleased and crinkly eyes of Abe Rownigan. 'Dad!' she cried, all but inaudible against the wind.

With his mittened hand, her father gestured to

her to take hold of his belt. He set off, still clutching Trouble, who looked very relieved about the improved travelling situation. Walking in her father's footsteps, Janey found the wind much more bearable, and within a very short space of time they were sitting next to a hole in the ice, giving each other the thumbs up and sliding down a steep icy tube into the world's southernmost Spylab.

As soon as they were all safely inside her father turned to Janey. 'What are you doing here? You know the conditions here don't suit you.'

'I know, but I had to see you. You're all right!' said Janey.

'I'm fine. Did you think something was wrong?'

'I got a message telling me, "Save our Sol".' Janey rattled out information as quickly as she could. 'And I'd just been to Sol's Lols HQ, which is completely overrun by Copernicus's spies operating out of this iceberg, and they've got a whole assassination team with a list, and I'm on it and I bet you're at the very top of it, and everything's really dodgy and worrying . . .'

Abe pushed back his hood, his sandy hair standing on end. 'Let's check in with G-Mamma.'

He crossed to his computer as Janey looked around the Spylab. It was just like the one under the wildlife park, except that everything – every workbench, stool, cupboard and shelf – was carved out of startlingly bright ice. In place of a refrigerator there was a series of hollows cut into the dug-out wall; the blacked-out sheet of ice opposite Janey obviously housed the Wower, as the door was otherwise identical to the one in G-Mamma's Spylab. And on every wall, almost filling the space, was a gigantic ice-plasma screen, displaying surveillance shots from various locations. 'Wow,' said Janey under her breath.

G-Mamma's face expanded to fill one of the screens.

Abe said, 'G-Mamma, Janey's here. Can you show me the "SOS" message?'

'I'll hold it up,' said G-Mamma. 'Someone's definitely written over the original message. Blondette thought it might be one of the twins.'

'The black stuff looks like their SPIsuits,' explained Janey quickly. 'It shimmers in the same way and it's got little feathers in it.'

Abe nodded. 'You're right. Rook's here; he's been busy at work, so I don't see how he'd have had time – perhaps Blackbird wrote it. We haven't been able to contact her for the last twenty-four hours.Can you run a test to see if the sample matches up with their SPIsuits?'

'Good idea. I'll get back to you,' said G-Mamma, and with that her face disappeared.

Abe turned to Janey, taking off his enormous outer padded jacket. 'It's pretty warm in here – only just below zero. At this thickness the ice is a better insulator than wood or fibreboard – it's how the Eskimos survive in igloos. Once you're out of the wind it feels much warmer, and where better than under the ground?' He smiled at her. 'Come and have a look around.'

They wandered around the Spylab together, opening ice doors and peering into cupboards. Abe then busied himself in the small ice kitchen, warming milk for hot chocolate in the microwave. Janey stared at one of the screens.

'Dad, what's with all the pictures of animals?'

Abe sprinkled brown powder into two mugs. 'I think it's time I filled you in on this mission. I told you at SPIcamp, didn't I, that there was something peculiar in the way the animals here were acting? Just look at Trouble.'

Janey glanced round, surprised. Sure enough, Trouble was perched on one of the highest refrigerator shelves, his back arched, all his hair on end and a steady quiver shaking him from the tip of his nose to the end of his tail. He was positively vibrating, with the beginnings of a snarl revealing the tips of his teeth.

'How weird! Come here, Twubs.' The cat stared down at her with his hypnotic emerald eyes but didn't move an inch. Even Abe couldn't persuade him to come down.

'Look at this,' said Abe, reaching for a remote control as he slid a hot chocolate across to Janey. 'This footage was taken just before an earthquake

137

in India.' The video clip was of a small herd of cows, veering this way and that as though an invisible whip was corralling them into place and quivering with the same intensity as Trouble.

'And this.' Abe pressed a button and the screen was filled with a news article, headed 'TSUNAMI – ANIMALS ESCAPE'.

KHAO LAK, Thailand – The tsunami claimed thousands of human lives, but in the animal world there appears to have been a sense of danger, almost a sixth sense that something was terribly wrong.

At the Khao Lak Elephant Trekking Centre, elephants Poker and Thandung started to panic – trumpeting and breaking free from their chains.

Their owner, Jong Kit, had never seen them behave in this way before. 'We couldn't stop the elephants,' says Kit.

Normally obedient animals, they ignored his commands to stop and ran for higher ground just five minutes before the resort where they'd been standing was destroyed by the tsunami.

Kit believes the elephants knew the tsunami was coming.

When the tsunami struck in Khao Lak, more than 3,000 human beings lost their lives in the region. But no one involved with the care of animals can report the death of a single one. The manager of the Khao Lak

National Park says all the animals went high into the hills, from where they have not returned. He believes not one perished in or around the park.

'We have not found any dead animals along this part of the coast,' he says.

Jong Kit's elephants' intuition was very lucky for four Japanese tourists who had climbed aboard them the morning of the tsunami. They all survived, carried on the elephants' backs to the hills.

'That's amazing,' said Janey. 'So you think the animals here know something terrible is on the way? Some kind of natural disaster?'

'Perhaps. Do you know, the Chinese city of Anshan managed to evacuate every person before an earthquake in 1975, all because of the way the animals were acting. Come on, there's more I want to show you.'

Janey nodded and followed her father through a set of ice doors that slid apart at the touch of his fingertip. From there Janey soon became confused as they walked from one corridor to the next. 'This place is like a labyrinth,' said Janey.

'That's right,' said her father. 'Not just a Spylab. It's a Spy-labyrinth. Bedrooms,' he pointed out, showing her the fur-covered slabs of ice in one of the rooms. 'Recreation room ... kitchen ... Antarctic laboratory ...'

Her father stopped, then pressed his fingertip to a spot on another ice-wall. Suddenly Janey found herself staring out at the gunmetal view, at a strange array of enormous, skittish animals.

'What's that?' she asked, pointing to a great black-headed bird, circling above and making occasional dives between icebergs. Its white body was as big as a large dog, and with its enormous wings it looked as though it could carry a couple of people on its back.

'That's an Arctic tern – one of the few birds that can survive here. Over there we've got a bunch of seals. Not so many leopard seals as we used to have – we don't know why exactly. Some of my scientists are looking into that. And over there . . . just beyond the seals . . . are some other birds that make this place their home.'

'Penguins!' squeaked Janey. 'But they're nearly as big as me!' Janey had always thought penguins were pretty cute, but these ones looked scary.

Abe laughed. 'Yes, not the little fluffy things you imagine they'd be. These are king penguins. And you can see they're not happy. The seals keep attacking each other, the terns have mostly left and the penguins keep shambling from one spot to another, pecking at each other. Something's wrong.' He shook his head, sighing. 'And then there are the ice-worms – they tunnel through the ice somehow, possibly using the solution they secrete from their skin to melt it, like a kind of antifreeze. They've never been found in Antarctica before, so what are they doing here?'

Janey was fascinated. 'Worms? That's what my sign said to begin with: Save our worms!'

'They're usually only found in the Arctic,' said her father. 'We want to find out more about them, but the poor things dissolve in temperatures above freezing, even body heat, so it's hard to do tests on them.'

The door closed between Janey and the bitter air outside, and she followed Abe back to the Spylab, deeply concerned. What was wrong with the animals? Trouble was acting oddly too, and now finding tunnelling ice-worms far from their usual home . . . Maybe they'd bored through from the North Pole like she had with her SPILL-Drills. And Janey suddenly remembered that someone else had once taken a great interest in her eSPIdrills and how she'd spun through the Earth – Copernicus himself. As the thought ran through her mind she felt as though the door had just opened again, so icy was the chill that ran through her . . .

Even more alarmingly, her father had already gone back into the Spylab, and between Janey and the door there now stood a formidable enemy, scaring Janey to the tips of her fleecy earmuffs.

It had scraggly eyebrows over demonic yellow eyes. It was as big as she was. And it was waddling straight for her.

14 zinc or zwim

'Dad,' Janey croaked, as the king penguin lumbered ever closer.

She looked behind her, but none of the doors to the rooms of the corridor were visible to the untrained eye. The only one she thought she possibly could open was the one to the outside. 'Probably just what it wants,' she thought desperately. 'Then it can round me up with its mates and they can peck me to death.'

Janey counted feverishly through her choices. Stab it with the titanium blade in her Gauntlet? No. It might be a killer, but she still couldn't bring herself to attack it first. Grappling in her pocket for her SPInamite, in the hope she could blast through into somewhere safe, she pulled out something else instead.

'Zinc cream?' she howled as the penguin backed her ever closer to the exterior ice door. Orange lettering leered up at her: 'ZINC OR ZWIM – for all those burning issues!' For a SPI-buy, it seemed pretty hopeless. 'What use is that?'

But it was all she had. Holding the open tube in front of her, Janey squashed it as hard as she could. The cream puddled ineffectually on to the corridor floor in a splat like a white cowpat. The penguin kept moving, side to side, swaying, getting ever closer . . .

Until something very strange happened. Where the zinc cream had landed, a small spiral of steam was now drifting up from the floor. She glanced down. There was a hole in the floor. And the penguin didn't seem to have noticed. Just as Janey's back touched the door, the penguin caught its flipper in the hole and fell flat on its face. Then, to Janey's bewilderment, it lay there, flapping and swaying as if it was still walking, beak down in the ice, as helpless as a baby.

Suddenly the Spylab door opened. 'Janey, what . . . Ah, I see you've met one of our SPUDs.'

'I thought you said they were kings?'

Abe grinned as he set the penguin back on its feet and pushed down hard on the top of its head. The waddling stopped. 'The real penguins are kings, but this is a SPUD – a SPI Underwater Detector. These little robotic devices swim around, sending back data, looking just like an ordinary penguin so enemies would never suspect them.'

'I thought it was attacking me,' said Janey quietly, wondering how she could ever have been worried

143

by the SPUD. Now that it was still it looked rather sweet, like a big toy.

'One of the Spylets might have sent him out, and you got in the way.' Abe turned the penguin around and patted its head again. 'We'll take him back in with us and reprogramme him.'

The SPUD reminded her of something. On their way back to the Spylab, Janey told her father about the Navy Seals, the underwater activity and the teams looking at geology and aeronautical engineering as well as assassination.

'I wonder what it is they thought they'd find? Metal, geology and aeronautical engineering?' Abe shrugged. 'They're going to be very disappointed. Still, that was good work, Blonde. I'll brief the others.'

Janey allowed herself a little smile as a thrill of pride ran down her spine, but it quickly disappeared as she entered the Spylab and found Titian Ambition lolling over one of the workbenches, casually chewing on an apple. 'Hi,' said Tish in a flat voice. 'What are you doing here?'

Abe pressed another invisible button in the ice wall and the loud hooting of a klaxon sounded throughout the labyrinth. 'Blonde has just completed a mission in Scotland which is of very great relevance to us. She's here to debrief and help out here if she can.'

'I thought we were doing OK,' said Tish, looking Janey up and down.

'We are, but Blonde has interesting news.'

There was a clattering at the door, and Janey looked around to see Alfie, Rook and a dozen or so scientists entering the lab. Alfie's eyebrows shot up at the sight of her; she smiled and gave him a tiny wave, which he didn't return. Too cool for that, thought Janey. In fact, he looked a little grey – perhaps he was sick, as Mrs Halliday had said. Rook looked her up and down in much the same way Titian Ambition had, while the scientists' brows puckered anxiously when they saw Abe leading Janey forward.

'Team, Blonde here has just been up to the Sol's Lols headquarters. There are enemy spies all over it.'

'Mainly under it,' said Janey.

Abe smiled. 'That's right. Divers and Navy Seals are burrowing under the building from beneath the lake, and apparently they have teams assigned to various things, only one of which makes any sense to me.'

He looked at Janey and she swallowed before saying, 'Assassination. They've got a list. They recognized me from it and tried to kill me. I don't know who else is on it, but the man said they'd sent all their assassins down here. They're around somewhere.'

A sombre hush fell across the room, and several pairs of eyes flickered back and forth. If the killers were in the Antarctic, they could be very close.

'We've had three scientists die already,' said

Abe, 'crushed to death in some unidentified clamp or vice. I know we'll get to the bottom of this. The most important thing is to work in pairs, cover each other's backs and stay calm. We can't discover anything if we're all running around terrified. You are trained professionals and can deal with whatever may come. Rook, how's the additional security coming along?'

Rook jumped up on a bench, swinging his legs. 'No problemo. All exterior doors have been reprogrammed for retinal scans and matched up to every eyeball in the place. Blonde, we'll have to have yours too.'

'My . . . eyeball?'

'Yes, your eyeball. Hand it over.' There were a couple of sniggers as Rook held out his hand. 'No, dummy, your *retinal scan*. And we'll need your fingerprint too – not your whole finger, just the print.' He smirked at Tish, and Janey lowered her eyes to the floor. Rook obviously enjoyed making her look an idiot, and Tish seemed to appreciate it too. He continued, 'We've got fingerprint scanners on all the internal doors. It'll be pretty difficult for anyone to get in if they're not meant to be here.'

'Good work.' Abe said nothing about Rook goading Janey, although he had looked carefully from one to the other as the exchange had taken place. He turned to Titian Ambition. 'Tish, how's the underwater surveillance?'

Tish patted the SPUD, now upright, bright-eyed

and turning its head left and right every so often, exactly like the king penguins outside. 'Nik here, and all his SPUD buddies, have been doing an ace job. So far there's nothing too out of the ordinary, apart from a bit of increased seal activity on an iceberg just a little east of here. They look perfectly normal though.'

'The ones in Scotland looked normal enough,' said Janey, 'but they were little mini-submarines with a spy in their belly. You should . . .' Janey paused. Judging by their expressions, Tish, Rook and a couple of the scientists thought she was speaking out of turn. She finished in a little rush. 'You should check them out again.'

To her relief, Abe nodded. 'Blonde is right. Can you get on to that, Tish? The two of you should work together on it. Let's debrief again at the end of the day.'

Clapping a couple of the scientists on the back, Abe dismissed them all. Janey sighed as Alfie and Rook left the room; she would have liked to talk to Alfie properly, but he wasn't here as her friend. He was here as a Spylet with a job to do. So was Tish. Janey sighed again. Even though she didn't really like Little Miss Ambition, if her father said they should work together, then they'd have to make every effort to do just that.

Tish stared at her for a moment, her frank green eyes taking in Janey's snowsuit and advanced Girl-gauntlet. After a few seconds, she obviously decided that Janey was up to the job, because she grinned and said, 'OK, Blonde. I'll show you how we programme the SPUDs. We keep them all in a room out in the labyrinth, out of the way of the real ones, who try to tear them apart. Of course it doesn't hurt them, but it makes a mess.'

Janey went over to where Tish was standing with the SPUD she'd thought was attacking her earlier. It blinked at her twice, and looked so innocent and sweet that Janey wanted to tuck it up in bed instead of sending it off into the icy Antarctic waters. Suddenly Tish got hold of the SPUD's beak and wrenched the two sections apart. Janey flinched as Tish talked her through the programming procedure.

'First, retinal scan to the back of the mouth – we have to be sure that it's one of us who's programming Nik.' Ramming one eye against the SPUD's open beak, Tish stared hard for a count of three and was rewarded with something that looked very strange – the whole of the top of Nik's head flipping backwards to reveal a small screen, a tiny keypad and a miniature joystick like Janey had seen on Alfie's computer games.

'Next,' said Tish, seizing the joystick between her thumb and index finger, 'select location. Look.'

Janey peered over her shoulder at the tiny screen. Shadowy images of icebergs, seals and the odd large, dark shape that she couldn't identify moved around the screen as Tish manipulated the joystick, until suddenly she found what she was looking for.

'Aha! There they are. Twenty-one . . . no, twenty-two seals that seem to have just moved home for no good reason. So this is our location. Now for the third step,' and she clicked on the coordinates that had appeared in a grid over the chosen site. 'And one last thing: don't forget to close his head. You get icy water in the mechanisms and they never work again.'

With that she flopped the top of Nik's head back into position, made sure it clicked into place and then stood well back. The SPUD swayed from side to side a couple of times and then waddled towards the door. 'They're preprogrammed so the doors open automatically,' said Tish and, sure enough, the ice door slid to one side as the SPUD approached. 'See you later, SPUD Nik!' yelled Tish.

Janey turned to her, puzzled. 'Don't you go with him? I mean, it?'

'Not if I can help it.' Tish rolled her green eyes. 'Do you know how cold that water is?'

'But we already know that new iceberg of seals may be suspicious – turning up out of the blue like that, just when I've seen a load of them in action in Scotland,' said Janey. 'If we wait for SPUD Nik to get back with information, it might be too late.'

'Blonde,' said Tish with a sigh, 'there are procedures, which you'd know about if you'd actually been chosen to come. If you don't like it, you could just go home. And take your freaky cat with you.' She turned

149

on her heel and, with a flick of her auburn curls, strode out of the room.

Trouble jumped down from his high perch up on the refrigeration shelves, looking highly offended. His tail-scarf had unravelled itself and then frozen solid, so it stood out like a flag in the breeze, and icicles had formed along his whiskers. 'She's right, Twubs, you do look a bit weird. And you're freezing. I think you have to keep moving while you're here.'

She tucked her quivering cat under her arm and thought about what she had just said. Keep moving. Yes. It was a bit of a dilemma. Either she followed procedures, and just waited for SPUD Nik to relay information back about the new seals, or she followed her instincts, which were telling her loud and clear that she already knew what those seals signified. If they were Navy Seals, then Copernicus's spies might be swarming all over the iceberg. It could even be how the killers were getting to and from her father's Spylab. She ought to BE there. But following her instincts could well get her into trouble or, even worse, sent home.

Janey dithered for about thirty seconds, then set Trouble down on the workbench. 'I'm going after Nik,' she told him. 'You stay here, keep warm and come after me if I'm not back in two hours.'

Trouble's emerald eyes stared right into hers, seemingly understanding every word. Blonde pulled her hood tight around her face, adjusted her fur-lined

Ultra-gogs and headed for the door. It stayed firmly shut. 'Argh! It doesn't recognize me yet.'

She stared at the ice before her for a couple of seconds and then smiled. 'There's more than one way through a door.' She pointed the Zinc or Zwim cream at the spot that Tish had just touched, and squirted. As soon as the ointment touched the ice it started to smoke, and before a minute had passed there was a hole the size of Janey's fist. She put her Girl-gauntlet into the gap, gripped the edge of the ice and pushed with all her might. To her great relief, the door slid open. She didn't have much time to catch up with SPUD Nik, so she grabbed her SPIFFInG and earmuffs – the only SPI-buys lying around on the counter nearby – and sprinted after him. With her Fleet-feet pounding against the floor, she raced along the labyrinthine corridors and skidded through the exterior door a couple of steps behind the SPUD.

'Hey, Nik, wait for me!' she yelled, but the wind captured her words instantly and sent them spinning away into air that was so cold it burned. The penguin robot was waddling determinedly into the darkness, so Janey ploughed on, forcing her way through the wind. She bumped into Nik's back just as he entered a crowd of real live king penguins.

They were quite terrifying close up, particularly as many of them came up to Janey's shoulder, and they shoved and tussled and pecked at each other in a slightly disturbing way. Hadn't her dad said that the penguins were acting peculiarly? She skulked along behind Nik, keeping close even when a couple glared at the SPUD suspiciously, until they had passed beyond all the live penguins and were travelling, just the two of them, across the ice cap.

It was only when they reached an edge that Janey suddenly took in the full enormity of what she was doing. This was the Antarctic. She'd come out here on her own, against orders. And all that stood between her and the icy black water was a robot penguin who was programmed to leap straight into it and seek out a random group of seals that could be innocent or could contain enemy spies. She looked back quickly, but could see nothing but whiteness. In the distance she thought she could hear a faint sound, almost like dogs barking, but it could just as well have been the wind playing tricks on her. Well, she'd gone this far, so she had better stick with Nik, who was now tottering towards the icy precipice. Trying to run into the wind, Janey leaped just as Nik's flippers hit fresh air and his whole body tipped forward into the chill waters. 'Wait for me!'

As Nik hit the surface, Janey straddled his back with just her feet trailing in the water. Even through her thick boots, the cold penetrated to her bones in seconds. She could hardly bear to think how cold she was going to be when Nik dived to gather his information . . .

But to her relief, he didn't dive. Instead he swam forward, flippers flapping, emitting the occasional beep from his beak. The seals were straight ahead, and that's what he'd been programmed to seek. The barking noise was getting louder – that must be the seals, thought Janey – and there was something else . . . a deep vibration, a noise that lodged itself in her ears like a trapped bee and then rattled uncomfortably through her body.

They had reached the seals' iceberg. SPUD Nik coasted around the outskirts until he found a suitably low edge to get on to the ice mass. They struggled out of the water together, Janey trying to get some feeling back into her feet as Nik careered left and set off again, resolutely seeking the information he'd been programmed to find. Janey followed, and saw they were heading for the centre of the iceberg.

Which was where she just managed to stop the SPUD from toppling head first into the biggest hole she had ever seen.

'Oh my word,' whispered Janey as she grabbed one of SPUD Nik's flippers just in time to stop him waddling over the edge. 'Oh no, oh no, oh no . . .'

Janey crouched behind Nik, hanging on to him with her Gauntlet to stop him continuing relentlessly on his fact-finding mission. His eyes had turned a startling white and were flashing madly as he snapped photos of the seals around them, who were shifting uneasily around the tunnel's circumference. Janey gasped as a wave of hideous nausea swept over her.

For the seals were guiding something to the edge of the hole. It was simply – and Janey knew there was no other way to describe it – a monster.

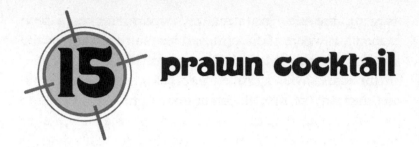

15 prawn cocktail

At first Janey thought the creature was a snake – an immense snake with the girth of a train, nosing its way forward slowly, coaxed on by the rough barks of the seals – but when she could bring herself to look again she could see that it was more like a gargantuan brown maggot. It moved by raising its middle up in a hump and then pushing its head forward, although whether it was its head or its tail was impossible to tell as it had no eyes, no face. The seals were having to lead it because it was blind.

'It's like a worm,' said Janey, horrified. 'One of those ice-worms Dad was talking about. But much, much bigger. Nik, take pictures!' She didn't actually know whether the SPUD could follow spoken instructions or do anything it hadn't been programmed to do, but it was worth a try.

The worm wriggled to the edge of the tunnel. Water pooled all around it and, as the creature nosed its way into the tube, Janey realized why. There was a deep watery rut where the worm had just slithered across the ice. And suddenly it became very clear what the purpose of the worm was. Janey edged as close as she dared to the edge of the tunnel, making sure she stayed hidden by Nik, whom the seals didn't suspect. She leaned over and peered into the darkness. This wasn't just a hole. It had no bottom. It was a tunnel – a vast, vertical tunnel. And the ice-worm was making it, burrowing into the ice and creating a bore-hole the size of its vast body with the ice-melting substance secreted from its skin.

Janey retched as the worm slithered into the hole. It was one of the most revolting things she'd ever seen, and she really wanted to turn Nik around, jump on his back, and find her way straight back to the Spylab. But something made her stop, something she noticed just as the tail end of the worm had disappeared from sight down the tunnel. All around the edge of it were familiar black shiny marks . . .

'Blonde!' said a voice in her ear, startling her so much that Janey fell forward and knocked SPUD Nik over.

'Don't let them see us. I hate seals, and they hate me!' hissed the red-haired spylet, and together they manoeuvred the SPUD back on to his penguin feet.

'What are you doing here?' said Janey. She had already worked out by their jerky movements – so like the bear at SPIcamp – that the seals were robotic, but she didn't really feel like telling Tish. Let her carry on being scared.

'Working in pairs, like we're supposed to!' Tish shook her head impatiently. 'Anything could have happened. That worm thing might have eaten you! Luckily I knew you were a bit renegade so I followed you. And man, that water is cold.'

They glared at each other for a moment, then turned back to look at the tunnel. Steam was rising eerily from its depths. 'I don't think it could eat me – it hasn't got a mouth. But look, it's blazing a tunnel through the ice.'

'What for?' whispered Tish.

Janey shrugged. That part was still a mystery, like the black marks around the rim. 'We have to go down there,' she said.

'No way!' squeaked Tish. 'Me and mineshafts do not go together. Besides, it's a vertical drop. And it isn't part of our brief!'

'We have to.'

'Do not.'

'We do.'

'Not.'

Janey sighed. Nothing was going to stop her getting inside that tunnel, but all this chit-chat was holding her up. Suddenly she thought of something. 'When my dad rescued you from the mineshaft when you were little,' she whispered, 'how did he do it?'

Crouched down behind SPUD Nik, Tish scratched a rough sketch in the ice. 'The mine went straight down like that tunnel, with Sinerlesse goons stationed all around the top,' she explained. She dug a little hole to the left of the mine. 'Your dad started here and tunnelled down to me at an angle to the main tunnel. Popped out right over my head, grabbed me and scooted back to the surface before they even realized.'

'Brilliant!' said Janey. 'Then that's what we're going to do.'

'Huh? What's this "we", Blonde?' Tish folded her arms crossly.

'Happy to do it on my own.' Janey glared back at her, equally stubborn.

Suddenly Tish grinned. 'Sometimes, Blonde, I like your style. OK then, if you're going to be all pig-headed about it, I'll watch out for you. I don't mind standing at the top of your tunnel, if you ever manage to make one . . . And I can send a SuSPInder line down for you if you get stuck.'

Janey was utterly surprised. She couldn't work this girl out at all. Sometimes she seemed incredibly difficult, and other times she said and did the nicest things. Could she trust her not to seal up the hole behind her? Her father did, that was evident. And she'd got out of worse scrapes before. 'All right,' she said slowly. 'Let's do it.'

They backed away, close to the edge of the iceberg

and out of sight of the seals, and Janey unravelled her SPIFFInG so it enveloped her from head to toe. Tish had never seen one before, but Janey interrupted her questions.

'It's easier to show you than tell you, and we don't have much time,' she said.

Tish nodded and pointed at the ice at their feet. 'OK, you need to start here. This is about as far away as your dad's tunnel was from the mineshaft.'

Janey pushed Nik ahead of her and stationed him to one side as protection from the seals if they should happen to follow them. Then, 'Watch this,' she said, and opened out the laces on her SPILL-Drills. For the first time she was going to have to tunnel in at an angle, not straight down, so she dug her right foot further into the snow, leaning on Nik so that she was at forty-five degrees to the surface. 'Press the little snowflake on my boot,' she told Tish, who did as instructed.

Janey saw Tish's eyes widen as she spun around in front of her once, twice, three and four times before she sped up so much that the other Spylet became just a blur of red. At rapid speed, Janey slid down into the ice, the SPIFFInG protecting her from the brain-numbing cold she knew surrounded her as she spun. Before too long the ice spinning around her gave way to water, and then earth strata, until they became interleaved with layers of lava and Janey knew from experience she would soon be hitting the Earth's metallic core.

She was spared the heart-stopping feeling of coming to a halt at the Earth's centre, however, as she suddenly found her feet were not making contact with anything. Fortunately this was a sign to the SPILL-Drills to end the journey, so Janey revolved ever more slowly until she finally came to a stop. Unlike the previous journeys, Janey didn't instantly clamber backwards, up and out of the hole. There was something different about this. It felt as though her feet were waving around in a vacuum. She normally popped out upside down on to flat ground, but this time, if Tish was right, she might just launch herself feet first into the tunnel and drop like a stone to the bottom of it.

It was with a great deal of difficulty that Janey managed to turn around inside the narrow tube she and her SPILL-Drills had just created, but eventually she was able to pop her head out like a mole from a hole, still wearing the SPIFFInG as though she was wrapped in cling-film.

'Eugh.' She drew her head back just in time to stop it being run over by a fat pink body. Was it another ice-worm? It looked different but she'd only had a split-second glance so couldn't really tell.

This time she eased her head out more cautiously and looked up and down. Her mouth opened in amazement, but no sound came out. This was just unimaginable.

Tish had been spot on. The tunnel was as straight

as a mineshaft – Titian Ambition would have had every reason to feel nervous about it – and it was absolutely vertical. Janey was far, far below the surface, but with her Ultra-gogs tuned in she could just see a white shape lowering itself into the tube. The ice-worm.

Janey was almost at the bottom and she could see that a solid tube structure connected the iceberg to the earth below. Somewhere in the excavation, other tunnelling creatures had taken over from the worm. These were every bit as repulsive, and Janey recoiled as a hard-shelled, maggot-like body the size of a large dog scrabbled across her face. There were dozens, maybe hundreds of them, burrowing and scraping and waving their hideous antennae around, stumbling into each other as they bored through the earth, ignoring the searing lava and glowing coals of the strata just below Janey to reach ever onward, right down to the solid metallic centre of the Earth.

The ones who weren't scratching a path through the Earth were blundering into each other on platforms anchored to the walls of the tunnel, feeding the waste material into a row of holes. They must lead to other tunnels, Janey realized, like the one she had just made herself. The weird creatures, who wouldn't have looked out of place in a giant's prawn cocktail, were clearing the tunnel and moving their scrap out of the way. Suddenly there was a commotion on one of the platforms opposite and Janey watched, horrified, as two

161

of the prawn-like animals tumbled sightlessly into the abyss, losing their footing as something – someone – stepped out of one of the side tunnels on to a platform. Their horrific screeches seemed to last for minutes, until finally they bubbled and stopped. The remaining creatures were now jostling around the figure that had stepped among them. Janey looked across to see who had disturbed them. And suddenly she wished she was far, far away. In fact, anywhere but here.

'Any more nonsense and you'll all join your friends,' the figure screeched. 'You're too slow! Move, and quickly!'

Janey would have recognized the voice anywhere. It was Copernicus. Her father's arch-enemy. Alfie's father. For the first time since she had known him, he was not disguised by the jagged and cruel Sun King mask, nor had he made any attempt to Crystal-Clarify himself into someone else. He wasn't even in the monstrous form that Janey had left him in when they last met, when she'd SPInamited him in G-Mamma's Wower. No, this was Copernicus as Janey had never seen him. He was tall and rail thin, with thick steel-grey hair tied back in a knot at the nape of his neck. What horrified Janey was the livid scar that cut across his mouth and the end of his nose, splitting his upper lip into uneven halves and exposing his raw gums. Janey shuddered. No wonder he had always hidden his face away.

She stared, unable to move, as a sightless creature

stumbled right across her path, then lunged for her. Suddenly Janey found her head smothered in revolting pink flesh. The SPIFFInG was being pulled off her head and she grappled for it desperately – if they punctured it, she would die in the suffocating heat.

'Aaaargh!' Raising her arms above her head, she pushed the creature off her with all the strength she could muster. The creature tipped, falling over her, scraping its feet along the tunnel to get a grip, and suddenly she found herself hurtling after it, out of her hiding place, and tumbling down the mysterious main tunnel. Her feet flailed helplessly as she clung on to the prawn-creature and it scrabbled to get a grip with its claws. The long laces of her SPILL-Drills melted the second they protruded from the SPIFFInG, Janey's body wriggled in space like a fish on a line, with a boiling soup of magma below her, and the fat creature whose leg she was holding screeched and struggled to keep hold of the wall of the tunnel.

'Ah, what . . . what do I do?' she gasped, staring wildly above and below her. The creature was slipping, unable to hang on . . .

A harsh, grating laugh echoed from the platform opposite her, metres away across the tunnel. 'Do? Well, I would have thought even you could work that out, Blonde. Getting in my way again, are you? Not this time, dear girl. This time,' he said, wheezing with arrogant laughter, 'you die!'

'No!' screamed Janey, as one of the great prawn's legs lost its grip on the wall and they both slipped further down the tunnel. 'Help me!'

But the misshapen sneer on Copernicus's face was so evil that Janey knew he would have no sympathy. He might not look such a monster as the last time she had seen him, but he still acted like one. Suddenly he gave a short laugh, and just as the creature lost another foothold and Janey swung out helplessly, crashing back against the tunnel wall, Copernicus turned around and headed out through the tunnel behind the platform.

He can get up his tunnel, thought Janey despairingly. Hers was blocked by the prawn-like creature that was currently the only thing between her and certain death. But the thought of Copernicus's tunnel sparked off an idea. She'd seen no sign of SPILL-Drills or SPIFFInGs, yet all the rubble tunnels would be at too steep an incline to simply walk up. 'He must have transport!' she gasped, trying desperately to get a better grip on the creature's leg with her left hand. She managed to take hold. Lifting the fabric of the SPIFFInG up out of the way, Janey pointed her free hand directly at the platform opposite, squeezed her middle finger with her thumb, and out came the heat-seeking missile with its tiny wire behind it.

Unfortunately the first heat it found was one of the creatures. Janey turned her head as it exploded, then she tugged on the line. It had caught in the metal grid of the platform. 'Now or never,' she said, and she let go of the creature's leg. Janey closed her eyes tight, not knowing if she was going to drop straight down into the lava, but the line held, and she felt herself swinging across the tunnel towards the exit Copernicus had just used.

'Missed.'

She was too low for the platform even though she was now on the right side of the tunnel, so Janey decided to use the only transport available to her, and she climbed on to the back of a passing mutant prawn. Unable to shake her off, it lumbered on and up to the platform, where she leaped off, already unwrapping her SuSPInder from her waist. She fed it out as quickly as she could then coiled it like a rope and flung it up the tunnel.

'Please work, please work, please work . . .' she prayed as the belt whistled ahead of her. And suddenly she knew it had. There was a clunk, the SuSPInder pulled taut, and Janey clung on for dear life as Copernicus's transporter yanked her towards the surface.

16 sons and saviours

From the angle Janey was at, she could see she was hanging beneath a compact SPIral staircase. As it flew up the angled shaft, Janey managed to edge her way up the SuSPInder, getting closer and closer to the capsule itself. When she was within a few metres of it, she fumbled with her free hand and turned up her SPI-Pod to hear what was going on inside. And her blood ran cold.

'Because it's magnetic,' Copernicus was saying, his voice almost gentle. 'It's what gives us gravity, and that's what I need.'

'What for?' whispered a hoarse voice.

'I've told you. It's for you, for us.' Now Copernicus sounded positively smug. 'Of course, the Earth will tip on its axis and be completely destroyed, but that's a small price to pay.'

'Pay for what?' mumbled the other voice so quietly that Janey could only just make out the words.

Copernicus sighed. 'I can see we'll have to adjust your wipe. When the time is right, my dear. When the time is right.'

The other voice spoke again, confused. 'What time?'

'Oh, go back to sleep,' snapped Copernicus.

'X-ray,' whispered Janey to her Ultra-gogs.

They complied immediately. From Janey's position underneath the transporter she could see two pairs of feet and the bottom of two pairs of trousers. One set of feet was long and narrow, encased in rigid shiny leather. Janey had seen those before. 'Copernicus,' she muttered.

But then she turned her attention to the other pair of shoes – chunky trainers with a small emblem on the bottom. 'Zoom,' she told her Ultra-gogs. The logo was clear . . . 'FF,' read Janey. Her breath caught in her throat. FF stood for Fleet-feet. She was looking at the shoes of a Spylet. It was Alfie.

Just then, Janey felt the transporter slowing. She looked around; they were travelling through ice again as she had at the beginning of her SPILL-Drill journey (and how long ago that seemed), so they must be close to the surface. She held on as tightly as she could as the spiralling stopped and waited to hear Copernicus and Alfie step out of the transporter. She was dangling rather precariously underneath: one wrong move and she could slip back down the shaft as if it was an enormous slide at a water park, out into the vertical tunnel again and end up fried at the bottom along with the unfortunate prawns. Wrapping the SuSPInder around her wrist, Janey edged up the tube until her head bumped the bottom of the capsule. After some delicate sawing with the titanium blade from her Girl-gauntlet, she had created a hole in the floor just big enough to climb through. She swung her legs over her head and through the gap, and pushed herself to her feet inside the capsule.

At long last Janey felt she was able to breathe freely again. She wriggled her way out of the SPIFFInG and posted it back through the hole in the floor. She heard it whoosh down the entry tube towards the tunnel. If Copernicus did ever find it, he would assume she had died as he'd intended. After carefully replacing the circle of metal in the floor to avoid suspicion, Janey listened at the capsule door before pressing the button to open it.

She stepped out into a terrifying labyrinth. It was very much like her father's, but as she'd seen in Copernicus's Spylab on a previous mission, his preferred colour was black. Obsidian walls winked at her, the only illumination coming from a sprinkle of tiny star-like lights on the ceiling. The atmosphere was thick with fear. Dread. Horror. Janey adjusted her Ultra-gogs to the night-vision setting and shuffled forward. Through the doorways around her she could hear odd snufflings and screeches, and the plink-plop of dripping icicles. 'That thing's going to sink into the floor again,' she heard someone complaining. 'Can't we stop it doing that?'

'Don't be daft,' replied a companion. 'That's exactly what he wants it for. Gives me the creeps.'

'What, the worm or the big C?' The first voice sniggered, and Janey recalled where she had heard that expression before – in Scotland, at the swimming pool.

'Don't you let him hear you saying that,' warned the companion, 'or you'll be following old wormy here down that infernal tunnel.'

'Right enough,' said the first voice thoughtfully.

Janey moved on until she heard other voices ahead, behind a closed door. She squatted down and pressed her ear against it, easily identifying Copernicus's nasal tones as they reverberated around the room. 'X-ray,' she said under her breath, and at once she could see beyond the door.

The Spylab room housed all the usual spy gadgetry, Wowers and so on, but to her surprise one whole wall was taken up with a glass panel behind which shifted millions of gallons of jet-black water. On another wall was a plasma screen showing family pictures of happier days – there was Alfie as a little boy, thick-haired and wise even as a toddler; Maisie Halliday before her teeth had been sharpened into points by the Crystal-Clarification Process; Copernicus himself, bending over to help Alfie along on his tiny tricycle, his face angled so that the camera only caught one side, the handsome side with its weight of grey hair and intense, intelligent eyes.

'You'll stay here until the planning's completed,' Copernicus was saying to Alfie, who was slumped against the counter. 'They won't miss you anyway, with the Halo-clone there. Keep you out of harm's way while we sort out that SPI group – and don't, whatever you do, stumble into the Supersizer. A giant Alfie would give the whole game away.'

So that was why Alfie had been looking grey when she'd seen him back at her father's Spylab. It wasn't him at all – it was a clone!

'Spy group?' Alfie himself was completely innocent – clueless, even. Copernicus must have thoroughly brain-wiped him.

Copernicus looked closely at his son. 'Maybe you should have a lie-down.'

He was walking towards the door. Janey lunged backwards, flat against the wall, just as the black-ice door slid open and Copernicus strode through it, guiding Alfie by the shoulder.

Janey watched, trying to keep her breathing silent, as they approached an almost invisible ice-door further along the corridor. Copernicus held Alfie's left hand up to a small panel to the side, and the door slid open. He gave his son a not-so-gentle shove. 'Go on, sleep it off. We'll talk when you've woken up. I'm going to see my . . . pets.' And to Janey's relief he strode away in the direction of the ice-worm stables she had passed earlier.

She ran into the Spylab. 'Come on, come on, there must be one here,' she said, scurrying from one table to the next. 'G-Mamma!' she said urgently into her SPIV. 'G-Mamma, where are you?'

'Oh, it's you, didgeridoo,' said the SPI:KE, looming upside down in the SPIV.

'You're in Australia again then?' said Janey.

'What if I am?' G-Mamma's inverted head looked like a potato with eyes.

'Never mind now,' said Janey quickly. 'I need the coordinates for Dad's South Pole Spylab.'

'Easy. S1,' said G-Mamma. 'Why . . . ?'

'Over and out.' Janey dropped the SPIV. There was the sharp click of footsteps in the corridor outside; if she wasn't quick she'd be caught in Copernicus's Spylab by the big C himself. Then suddenly she found what she was looking for. With a split second to spare, Janey pressed the Satispy remote, now programmed for S1, and dropped the control as soon as her hands started to disintegrate. The last of her cells disappeared as the footsteps reached the door and she slipped unseen into the atmosphere.

Moments later she reassembled in a pleasantly white Spylab. Trouble, seeming much more himself, ran across and leaped into her arms. Janey gave him a squeeze. 'Hello, Twubs. It's nice to see a *normal* animal, I can tell you.'

'And is it nice to see me too?' said a deep voice. 'It's certainly a relief to see you.'

Her father was sitting at one of his benches, nursing a cup of coffee and zooming in to some images on the ice-plasma screen. 'You went off without saying goodbye.'

Janey winced. It sounded as though she was in trouble. Again. 'Dad, I know I shouldn't have gone, but you've always said I'm sort of instinctive, and I just had to do it. And Tish was with me – sort of.'

At that moment Tish walked into the room. 'I'm sorry, sir, I still haven't . . . oh, there you are!'

'Tish came and told me your plan when Trouble found his way out to her. He'd obviously come to fetch you,' said her father. He was trying to sound stern, but Janey was sure she could see the hint of a smile in his brown eyes.

'I did tell him to do that. Thanks, Tish.'

The red-haired girl shrugged. 'I told him it was all your idea, so if we've been naughty, you're the one who gets sent home.'

'Fair enough,' said Janey quietly. She really hoped it wouldn't come to that as she had some very important news to pass on. 'Dad, could I have a word?'

Her father nodded to Tish, who sighed and left the room. Then he turned to Janey. 'What have you found out?'

Trying hard not to gabble, Janey said, 'Copernicus is building a tunnel from the Antarctic to the centre of the Earth. He's nearly finished it, and when he does he's planning to tip the world on its axis and that will destroy the whole planet. He's got all these freaky creatures working for him, tunnelling – a massive maggoty ice-worm and these huge prawns.'

'Volcanic shrimps,' said her father, nodding. 'Mutated, I expect. He must have some multiplying device to make small creatures gigantic.'

'He mentioned it! A Supersizer or something. These prawns are huge, and really disgusting,' said Janey. 'But Dad, here's the scariest thing: he's got Alfie. The one here is a clone.'

Her father turned white and he closed his eyes in horror. 'Of course,' he said under his breath. 'No wonder the killer's been able to get in here – the clone must have been letting them in. I'll get the Alfie-clone rounded up somewhere safe. And I'd better check the others too.'

'That's not the worst of it, Dad.' Janey paused, unsure how to tell her father what she'd overheard. 'He's brain-wiped him so Alfie doesn't know what he's doing, and he's obviously planning somewhere for them both to escape to when he . . . destroys the world.'

'The madness has seized him completely.' Abe put his head in his hands. 'We have to find him and destroy him before he kills us all. I'll go immediately, if you give me the location.'

'But if he sees you he'll kill you, or his assassins will. And he'll kill all the rest of us, if you're not here to fight for us.'

'What choice do I have?'

Janey watched as her father stood up and started gathering equipment. A plan had just occurred to her – a slightly mad plan, and a risky one, but one that meant she could get to Copernicus, alone, without anyone being killed. If she could destroy him once and for all, they could accomplish everything they needed, all at once.

'There is another way,' she said quietly.

Her father looked at her, chewing his lip, then said, 'I'm listening.'

Janey could hardly believe what she was about to say. Only three people, to her knowledge, had ever done what she was about to suggest, and they were all superSPIs. But it was the only way.

She lifted her chin. 'Dad,' she said, 'I want you to Crystal-Clarify me.'

17 clarification

To begin with, her father refused outright. 'You know what a risk it is. I'd have to inject your cells to make them traceable, freeze you solid and then reform you in another body. A million different things could go wrong.'

'You've done it,' said Janey. 'You've been a swimming pool, a frozen swan and now this whole new person, and you're still OK.'

Abe rubbed his chin. 'That's a good point. I could do it again this time.'

'No!' Janey knew her father had been weakened by too many Clarifications and super-long Satispy trips. 'You're too . . . big,' she said, 'and too important to the rest of the team – to the whole of SPI! It makes more sense for me to do it.'

'If something went wrong, I could never forgive myself, Janey. And how would we explain it to your mother?'

Janey gulped a little as G-Mamma's voice suddenly boomed out into the room. 'Righty almighty: your mum thinks you're asleep in your jim-jams, Blonde, and yet you've already been right about those birdy SPIsuits and goodness knows what else.'

'Was I?

'Tested positive,' confirmed G-Mamma. 'The writing on the placards was done by one of the birds, and it's more than likely to be the same stuff you saw at Sol's Lols.'

'So I have to go!' pleaded Janey.

'And what will we tell your mother?' said G-Mamma. '"Hi, Clean Jean. Your daughter's been shot in the Arctic"?'

'Well, I—' started Abe, but Janey interrupted him.

'Antarctic,' she corrected.

'Whatever. Shot somewhere cold.'

'G-Mamma,' said Abe to the video image of G-Mamma on the ice-plasma, pink-cheeked and fanning herself with a hand laden with opal rings and bracelets, 'you're Janey's SPI:KE – if you say no, then . . .'

Suddenly Janey felt cross. Her father was doubting her ability to cope all over again, her SPI:KE was so busy in Australia these days that she didn't really have a right to an opinion but was definitely about to give one, and even Tish was hovering outside the door ready to stick her oar in.

'Look, all of you,' she said loudly, 'I'm the only

one qualified to do this. I know Alfie best, so I won't give anything away by doing something . . . un-Alfie-ish. He might even think I'm the clone. I know my way around Copernicus's labyrinth and Dad's here to make sure it's the best Crystal Clarification ever. It makes sense that I should do this, and I don't care what any of you say.' Janey glared around the room. 'Sorry, but that's what I think,' she mumbled.

G-Mamma's face broke into a broad grin. 'Well, girly-girl, all I can say is that old Copper Knickers had better watch out. Oh, and this,' she added, shouting, 'Didgeridoo, Berty-Bert-Bert!'

An aggrieved voice in the background muttered, 'You crazy Sheila,' then a deep sonorous rumbling started up from somewhere behind G-Mamma. She bopped her head in time, waving her arms above her head.

'She's a spylet on ice, and a spylet twice –
Old Copper's gonna find his Knickers knot-ted.
She's a spylet true, Crystal-Clarified too,
And she's gonna end whatever Knickers plot-ted.
Oh yeah . . . oh yeah . . .
Give it up . . . give it up . . .'

'Um, that's great, G-Mamma,' said Abe as the SPI:KE shimmied off the screen. 'You carry on, and we'll start the process.'

'Okey-doke, Bossman! Take care, Blonde,' she yelled, and the screen went blank.

For a long moment her father stared at Janey, holding her hands. 'Are you absolutely sure?'

'My instincts tell me it's right.'

'Then we have to get on with it.' Abe hugged her fiercely for a moment, then led her through to a small surgical-looking laboratory behind one of the ice-walls. He looked carefully left and right before closing the door. 'Nobody must know about this,' he said. 'For your safety, and to make sure the process remains a secret.'

He filled a syringe with a bright orange substance, and Janey tried not to look at the size of the needle. 'I promise you this is the only part of the Crystal Clarification Process that hurts,' said Abe as he injected the tracer into Janey's arm. She winced and held the side of the chair – it was definitely the worst injection she had ever, ever had, but if that was as bad as it was going to get, then there wasn't too much to be scared of. Apart from getting stuck in Alfie's body, or killed by Alfie's father . . .

Janey felt a tingle spread throughout her body as the tracing solution entered every one of her cells. Then, on Abe's instruction, she lay down on the ice bench in the middle of the room. Her father retreated behind a partition. 'You won't be very aware of anything when you're completely frozen. The best thing is to try to sleep. It takes quite a long time. And then when you come to, hopefully you'll be Alfie.'

'Dad, I . . .' I love you, she wanted to say, but that sounded as though she believed this was goodbye, that the process wouldn't work. 'I trust you,' she said instead.

He nodded briefly, his brown eyes welling up a little, and then he stepped into a cubicle and turned down the temperature in the surgical laboratory. The coldness seeped inside Janey's SPIsuit immediately, and she tried to stay still as a deep, jerky shivering overtook her body. Above her she could see a three-dimensional laser image of Alfie, sometimes as he looked in his SPIsuit, and sometimes just his skeleton, revolving like a chicken on a spit. Millions of red lasers spanned the ceiling in a cat's-cradle version of Alfie, blinking and altering and shifting so that Janey's eyes grew tired watching them. By now she had passed beyond shivering to occasional whole-body spasms, where her feet and head would remain on the table but the whole of her body in between would convulse as though she had just had thousands of volts fed through her.

'It doesn't hurt though,' thought Janey dreamily. 'Not too bad really. What am I doing here again?'

She had been warned that the brain-freeze would cause her to get confused, but it had taken such a grip that Janey couldn't remember what she was supposed to be confused about. 'Never mind

– sleep, sleep,' she told herself. Her breathing slowed, her body became still ... and Janey dreamed: of happy families playing on bikes, of strange creatures swimming around her in the depths of the ocean, of Titian Ambition staring green-eyed with envy through the window – or were they just her normal eyes – and finally nothing.

Janey came to with a start. 'What's the time?' she said, for no particular reason, other than that she had a pressing awareness somewhere inside her that there wasn't much time left, that she had to get on with something. What was it exactly?

And then, slowly, she remembered. She opened her eyes. The spinning laser image above her head was still there, but it was no longer Alfie she was looking at. Instead she stared right into her own face, which tipped away so she could see her Blonde ponytail and then suddenly, horribly, the outline of her own skull. She closed her eyes again quickly. Did that mean it had worked?

'Sit up slowly,' said her father's voice. 'You'll get dizzy if you try to move too quickly.' Abe took her arm gently and helped her into a sitting position, his expression full of admiration. She smiled at him, feeling her lip curl into an unfamiliar shape – Alfie's one-sided sarcastic grin – and she stared at her dad in wonder.

He nodded. 'Yes, it worked perfectly, Janey. Or should I say – Al Halo.'

Helping her to her feet, he guided Janey to a heavily polished sheet of ice in one corner. It was staggering. Janey would not have believed what she was seeing if it hadn't been for the feeling of her father's arm around her shoulders; in the the reflection her father was standing protectively next to Alfie Halliday. Yes, definitely Alfie in every way, from his trainers-and-denim-silk SPIsuit with zips, through his new improved, acid-spraying Boy-battler, to his silver-rimmed Gogs covering chocolate-brown eyes and his thick chestnut hair. Janey's hands flew to her cheeks in shock, but she thumped herself in the temple with the Boy-battler and staggered sideways against her father.

'Steady,' he said, holding her up. 'You'll get used to it. Quickly, I hope. I think it's time we sent you on your way.'

Janey took a few deep breaths. 'I'll be ready soon – oh!' It shouldn't have surprised her, but it sounded so odd to hear Alfie's voice come out of her mouth. 'Just give me a moment.'

Her father stood back while she walked around the room, getting used to Alfie's feet and his casual saunter. After about a minute she turned to face him. 'I'm ready.'

They stepped out into the main Spylab. Trouble ran over to her immediately – clearly he wasn't fooled by her unusual appearance. Rook and Tish were keying information into the computer and glanced up. This would be the real test. 'Halo, we need your retinal scan,' said Rook.

Janey looked at her father. Would the details be correct right down to the eyeballs? He nodded imperceptibly and Janey crossed over to the counter. Tish ignored her completely as she said to Abe, 'The penguins are really jumpy at the moment, and most of the seals have left. There's something upsetting them, that's for sure.'

'I have an idea what it is. I'll go and have a look,' said Abe. 'All done there, Alfie?'

Having pressed her – or rather Alfie's – eye against a tall upright camera, Halo's retinal scan was completed, so Janey nodded and followed Abe through the labyrinth to the exterior compound. Tish was right: the penguins were skidding anxiously from one place to another, hardly able to stay upright, jumping into the water and then flinging themselves back out on to the ice. Meanwhile only two seals remained, and they were snapping at each other and any penguins who happened to get too close.

'No time to lose,' shouted Abe over the wind. 'Are you ready?'

Janey gave him an awkward thumbs up, hampered by Alfie's Boy-battler, and then laughed as she saw one of the penguins staggering towards them. 'SPUD Nik!'

'Take him with you,' said her father. 'He's been programmed and he'll keep us informed of what's going on.'

Suddenly aware of what she was taking on, fear hit Janey in the stomach. She held on to her father for as long as she dared, and then stepped to the edge of the ice.

'You first, SPUD Nik,' she said in a sardonic, Alfie way. The SPUD tipped into the water; Abe lowered Janey in after him, and she stood on the penguin's back like a surfer as Nik pulled away across the freezing water. This was it. She was on her way.

It took about eight minutes of SPUD-surfing to get across to the suspiciously seal-covered iceberg. For a moment Janey thought she should hide behind the penguin as she had done earlier, but she quickly realized there would be no need. Alfie was Copernicus's son – there would be strict orders from on high that he should not be harmed. In Alfie's body, even Jane Blonde was well protected.

She trotted quickly around the gaping tunnel to the Earth's centre, following the slimy, half-melted tracks of the ice-worm. 'Just as I hoped,' she said, when she was led straight back to the labyrinth. But it was not going to be straightforward. The bearded spy and the assassination group leader were on guard duty at the exterior door. Janey took a deep breath and walked right up to them.

'Business?' barked the bearded man, holding a gun up to Janey's face.

'Duh, the big C's son?' she replied, staring back at him cheekily as she was sure Alfie would do.

'Blimey, it is,' muttered the assassination group leader. 'Sorry, Mr . . . Al . . . um . . .'

Janey grinned. This was actually quite fun. 'You can call me C-Junior,' she said. 'Are you going to let me in?'

'Oh, sure, sure. And the . . . penguin?'

'It's my SPUD,' said Janey. She had no idea whether anyone but SPI had SPUDs, but the two guards were too in awe of Alfie to stop her anyway. 'It comes too.'

The door slid open and Janey stepped through. Once again the oppressive darkness made her falter and she paused for a moment to get her bearings, then remembered she had all the direction she needed right by her side. All she had to do was follow Nik, who had been programmed to get her to Alfie's room. Within a few moments she had been led to the correct door and, remembering what Copernicus had done with Alfie's hand, Janey removed her left glove and held her fingertip to the tiny panel to the left of the door. It ground into action immediately, but instead of feeling pleased, Janey felt incredibly anxious. So far it had been quite easy, but what was coming next would be one of the most difficult things she would ever have to do.

The door opened fully. Alfie was lying on the bed, staring with dull eyes at the ceiling. He sat up, glancing at the door, and then got to his feet as his eyes adjusted in the dim light. For the first time he saw who had just come in the door. Himself.

'What are . . . ?'

'I'm really, really sorry, Alfie,' said Janey. 'But you'll blow everything if you walk in unexpectedly.'

And – *wham!* – she planted the Boy-battler firmly between his eyebrows, knocking her best friend out cold.

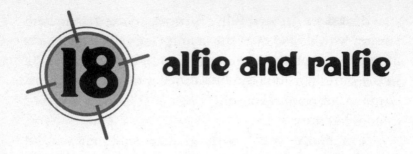

18 alfie and ralfie

Janey dragged Alfie's inert body back to the bed, levered him under the blankets and covered him up, leaving just enough of a space at the top to stop her friend from suffocating. The room was so dark, like everything else in the light-deprived labyrinth, that if someone did manage to open the door they would assume the room was empty.

With Alfie out of the way, she was safe – or at any rate, safer – to enter the Spylab and confront Copernicus. And not just confront, but destroy him. How she was going to do that she wasn't quite sure. Acid-spray him with Alfie's Boy-battler? It occurred to Janey that she didn't really know exactly how the Battler worked. She could just as easily end up squirting acid all over herself or trying to kill him with a hairnet. Was that what Alfie had said? Some kind of net anyway . . .

The best thing to do was not to think about it,

she decided. Trying to look more relaxed than she felt, and with SPUD Nik swaying from side to side on his flippers, she held her finger up to the Spylab code pad and waited for the door to recognize Alfie. When nothing happened, she did it again. The door refused to budge. It was her first hurdle, and Janey wasn't sure what to do next. If she started melting doors with Zinc or Zwim cream, like she had in the white Spylab, Copernicus would immediately be suspicious that an intruder was in his facility.

As she paced in front of the door, however, she spotted something that Alfie's door hadn't had – a code keypad. Of course! she thought. Only Alfie can get in his room, but anyone with the right fingerprint and code can come in here.

Pushing up her sleeves, she stared more intently at the little image on the LCD screen. 'Look, Nik, it's you,' she said, pointing out the picture of the king penguin that was blinking on and off on the display. The blinking was getting more rapid, she noticed. The keypad would probably be on a timer – any delay and she'd be locked out permanently, alarms would go off and she might as well be marauding up and down the corridors screaming, 'Jane Blonde is here!'

'Concentrate, Blonde,' she told herself. The penguin was flashing so rapidly now that it was giving her a bit of a headache – maybe Alfie was prone to migraines – but she did have time to notice that to the left of the bird figure there were three dashes. 'A three-letter word that means penguin? Short for penguin? Or . . . Or . . . I know!'

Just as the penguin was starting to flicker off and on continuously, Janey keyed in the word 'SUN'. 'Please be right,' she whispered. It was. The door swept open, giving Janey a view of the whole Spylab. It was a good job she knew how vain Copernicus was, and what his other name had been. A *king* penguin with a three-letter word before it meant it had to be 'sun' for Sun King, the alter ego that Copernicus had once created.

She walked tentatively into the lab, SPUD Nik tottering along beside her. 'Hello?' she called in as Alfie-like a manner as possible. There was no reply. Janey pushed the button to make the door close and issued a new instruction to Alfie's Ultra-gogs. 'Floodlight.'

To her delight, both rims extended up her forehead, joined together into one big circle, and lit up, pouring a halogen-white light all over the lab from what now looked like a miner's lamp on her head. 'That's better.'

It was very much easier to see. The Spylab, though black, was actually very similar to her father's and G-Mamma's, but she still took the time to walk around it methodically, trying to memorize where everything was in case the lights went out again. She approached the door behind the plasma screen with the cheery family photos on it: in her father's lab, this was where Crystal

Clarification took place. She assumed this would be the same, as Copernicus had certainly used the process before, but to her surprise when she looked into the room she could see a 3-D laser cast, like the one of Alfie that had been rotating above her when she had Crystal-Clarified. It was Copernicus, projected straight through the wall from the photograph on the other side of it. Janey paused, confused. Had Copernicus Crystal-Clarified himself into . . . himself? It didn't make sense. There was no sign of any needles or Clarification tables – just a small round platform under the laser cast. 'Weird,' she said.

She remembered something else that was weird, and headed over to the immense glass tank filling up the whole of one side of the room. With her floodlight angled against the glass, Janey could see a little way through the water. The tank appeared to be completely empty.

Janey shrugged, turning away from the tank. Then as she put out her foot, Alfie's trainer connected with something oily on the floor and she found herself skidding across the lab. Dusting herself off, she went back for a closer look. It was water from the tank, as she'd suspected, but mingled in with it was something else – something dark. Nearby was another black stripe of some shiny liquid substance. 'Just like the bird SPIs' suits again!'

Janey was sure of it now. A double agent was operating in their midst. It had to be Rook. He must have been up at Sol's Lols, informing the big C's spies. He'd gone to her house to try to persuade her that her father was in danger, not Alfie. And pretty recently he'd been in Copernicus's black Spylab, consorting with the enemy, getting his orders. 'So that's how Copernicus got hold of Alfie,' she thought. Rook had betrayed him. And by betraying Alfie, he had betrayed them all.

'SPUD Nik, come here,' she said to the penguin. Thankfully Alfie's eyeball had already been registered for SPUD programming, so she wrenched open Nik's beak, stared at the back of his mouth and waited for his head to flip open. She wasted no time keying in the S1 coordinates and speaking directly into the screen. 'Rook was in here – the black stuff from his suit is all over the floor. Don't trust him. I think he betrayed Alfie.' Then she slammed home the top of Nik's head, spun him around and sent him waddling back to her father's Spylab.

She wasn't a moment too soon. As she watched the yellow-eyed bird lumber out of sight, a figure appeared in the open doorway. For a moment Janey's heart dropped to the bottom of her boots – Copernicus had caught her, red-handed, snooping around in his Spylab! But then she looked at her boots and noticed they were, in fact, trainers. Alfie's trainers. He wouldn't suspect anything at all.

'Better for a little sleep?' As Copernicus walked

over to her, Janey had to prevent herself from recoiling at the sight of his evil face and his nasty gimlet eyes.

How would Alfie answer? 'I s'pose,' she ventured.

'Good,' said her arch-enemy, turning his back on her to study something on the computer screen. 'Hopefully you'll be less sluggish at the computer. Come and help me out here. Find out how aeronauticals are doing.'

Janey drew in beside him at the computer, the closeness to him nearly making her shudder. What did he want from her? Her fingers hovered over the keyboard. She couldn't destroy him just yet – she wasn't prepared. But maybe the computer would tell them something significant. 'I . . . I don't know . . .'

'Suns and solar systems, boy, I'm going to have to get that brain-wiper checked out! It's not meant to make you stop functioning altogether. Remember what I told you the other day,' said Copernicus with a weary sigh. 'Password first, then into Departments, Aeronauticals, Update.'

Janey tapped in the words as instructed with her free left hand, hoping desperately that the password was 'SUN' again. It was. A drop-down menu led her into Departments and then Aeronauticals, and then she clung on to the edge of the countertop for a moment as the Update command brought up an image she could hardly believe.

Copernicus was building a rocket. Or rather, he had *built* a rocket. As high as a four-storey building, it had swarms of technicians tinkering with it from a series of platforms encircling it. That was why he needed aeronautical engineers . . .

'Focus on the door,' snapped Copernicus.

Janey jumped. She'd been so engrossed in the pictures before her that she'd almost forgotten where she was. 'Door,' she said, nodding, pulling down menus as fast as she could.

'No, use the mouse!' Copernicus was getting ever more irritated. Why doesn't he just do it himself? thought Janey.

'Would it be quicker if you did it?' she said, relieved to hear Alfie's voice coming out from between her lips.

It was clearly the wrong thing to say. 'Don't get smart with me, boy,' snarled Copernicus. 'Just pan over to the door.'

He bent past her, pointing to the space at the bottom of the rocket that was meant to be the door, so that Janey had to crane her neck to see past him. His thick steely ponytail looked like a judge's wig from the back, and Janey was just about to allow herself a small smile when she remembered something. She stole another glance at the back of Copernicus's neck. There was nothing wrong with it. Nothing at all.

Which meant that something else was very wrong

indeed. For as long as she had known Copernicus, even with his sun mask on, she had been aware of the terrible injury to the back of his neck caused by a poor attempt at Crystal Clarification, almost as if someone had torn a second grotesquely disfigured mouth into the top of his spine. But now the skin was unbroken, the flesh neat and normal. Perhaps he's had surgery, thought Janey. But if he had, why would he not have corrected his face at the same time? And where was the scar?

'Focus!' barked Copernicus.

In her confusion, Janey reached for the mouse, but he was still in the way. She would have to touch him, couldn't help but touch him as she nudged his arm out of the way to do as he instructed. To her disgust and horror, however, she didn't need to move his arm. Her hand simply passed straight through it.

Janey couldn't help a tiny gasp escaping through her lips. He wasn't real. 'You're a SPIRIT!' she blurted.

His head whipped round suspiciously. 'A Retrospectre,' he corrected. 'I can't appear to you in my current form, so I've chosen this image from the past to recreate myself, just for you.'

She was still looking shocked, she realized, so she tried to pull herself together. So that was why there was a laser image buzzing in the room behind the photo! That was how Copernicus was presenting himself, to his son at least, which meant that the real Copernicus could be anywhere, looking like anything or anyone.

'Yeah, thanks,' she said in the most Alfie-ish way she could think of.

But Copernicus's eyes had suddenly narrowed. 'All at once you've remembered something from your Spylet past, my son? Even after being brain-wiped.'

Janey faltered – she'd forgotten that Alfie was struggling to recall his own name at the moment. 'Just . . . just came back to me.'

'And you brought to mind the password to get in here and use the computer when you've never been able to remember it before.'

He was becoming suspicious. Janey waved her arms about, raising one side of her lip in Alfie's lopsided grin. 'Nah, I'm the clone, aren't I?' she said.

For a long moment Copernicus stared at her, the steel of his eyes boring into her own. Then he said quietly, 'Fine. Just go into Department, Rooms, A1.'

Inwardly sighing, Janey turned back to the keyboard, found the drop-down menu for Department, then selected Rooms, and A1. As soon as she hit the button though, she wished she hadn't. There, clearly outlined by the ultraviolet light, was the inside of Alfie's bedroom and, more worryingly, the sleeping form and face of Alfie Halliday, Copernicus's son.

Janey hit Escape quickly, then said, 'Oh, sorry, didn't mean to do that . . .'

But Copernicus was already on to her. 'The clone dissolved two hours ago. Still haven't sorted out that Cinderella gene. And my son is tucked up in bed. So who are you exactly?' he hissed. 'Blonde . . . or her confounded father? Well, you've just made my job very easy.'

He reached out a sinewy hand to grab her wrist. Janey recoiled, then shouted with relief as his fingers passed straight through her arm. 'You're a Retro-spectre!' she cried. 'Just a ghost. You don't have a body!'

'We'll see about that,' screamed Copernicus. 'Spylab lockdown!'

The doors were voice-activated; the second the last letter had left his ghostly severed lips the doors snapped shut. From what he'd said, his actual body was close enough to do Janey some real damage. She had to get out.

She ran for the door as the muddy water in the vast glass tank began to bubble and boil. 'Sun King!' she yelled in Alfie's voice, desperately holding up her finger to the keypad. It was useless, and the hologram of a Copernicus memory laughed his horrid metallic laugh as a thunderous swish and boom echoed out from the tank. The glass was creaking, bowing under the enormous pressure of the thrashing activity behind it. Janey glanced behind her as Copernicus laughed maniacally; any second now the glass would shatter, and whatever was behind there would flood out into the lab, grabbing her, reaching for her, completing one of the hits on that assassination list . . .

She spun back to the door. Which finger was the acid spray? Janey had no way of remembering – hadn't Alfie been rather vague about it himself? – so she stood well back and squeezed her left hand tight around all the fingers of her Boy-battler at once.

All the functions were activated together. A fine mist of putrid yellow acid spurted from her index finger, evaporating the lower half of the door, the floor below it and the toecap of the guard who had appeared behind it. Janey watched the bare toe zoom away down the corridor as the rocket launcher caught the enemy spy full in the stomach and propelled him backwards towards the exterior door at great speed. The rocket detonated at the back door and cold air rushed back in along the corridor. Janey started to run but found herself tangled in the web of the dragnet which had also been released from the Boy-battler. There was a sound of ice cracking, and she thought it must be the packed ground outside, split apart by the rocket, but then realized it was coming from behind her. The glass in the tank was shattering. Janey fumbled, terrified, for the only SPI-buy still remaining in Alfie's Boy-battler – a titanium blade just like her own. In seconds, even as she heard the tank splintering and gallons of icy water – and heaven knew what else – crashing to the floor, she sliced through the clinging strands of net, chucked the whole thing behind her and sprinted down the corridor.

She was almost at the back door, almost free, when she remembered something. 'Alfie!' She couldn't leave him here. Spinning on her heels she Fleet-footed back down the corridor, sloshing through ankle-high water, then held up Alfie's finger to his door keypad and hurled herself into the room, hauling the door closed behind her as she body-rolled towards Alfie's bed.

'Huh?' he said blearily. 'Hello, er, *me*.'

'I'm not me, I mean, you.' Janey grabbed his arm. 'Alfie, there's no time to explain. Just trust me. We have to get out of here.'

She hauled him to his feet, aware that they must look like twins, and headed for the door, but even as she opened it she realized there would be guards, perhaps even Copernicus himself, gathering outside.

'This way,' she puffed, dragging Alfie to the wall beside his bed. Her own Boy-battler acid had all been used up, so she lifted Alfie's right hand and pressed hard.

'Ow, you hurt me. Or . . . I hurt me . . .' he said pitifully, but Janey didn't give him any time to complain. Instead she bent him almost in two and pushed him through the hole in the wall before following him and pointing and squeezing his hand to fill the hole with the dragnet from his glove, where it clung like a spider's web to the ice.

But it was only when she turned around, and found herself in a frozen cave confronting an enormous body like a deep pink marshmallow, that Janey understood what she had done.

'Oh no,' she said.

They were in a worse mess than ever. Right next to Alfie's room, it turned out, was where the ice-worms were stabled.

19 melting monsters

There was no way back. Already there were shouts and muffled thuds behind them in Alfie's room. And yet there was no way forward either – every inch of the vast chamber before them was taken up with the pulsating, revolting, blood-coloured body of the ice-worm.

'Oh!' Alfie reached out a hand. 'A bouncy castle.'

'Don't touch it!' Janey snatched his fingers back. 'It has stuff on it that melts ice – it might just melt us too.'

'Can I go back to bed then? Please,' said Alfie plaintively.

Janey shook her head. She had to think. There must be some way out, but short of blasting the thing apart with the rocket launcher, which might well leave them dead too, the only way seemed to be to go back and confront whoever or whatever was in Alfie's room, blundering about in the dark and trying to poke its way through the dragnet.

The ice-worm, although it couldn't see, could clearly sense their presence. To Janey's surprise it seemed to be trying to back away from them, but the space in the cavern was so tight that it couldn't move. In fact, by struggling it was actually getting closer to them. 'Why doesn't it want us close to it?' she wondered.

And then, with a brilliant flash of light in her brain, something occurred to her, something her father had said. It was impossible to do tests on ice-worms because . . . because what? 'They dissolve with the heat – human body heat! Yes!'

The next second she was ripping off her Boy-battler and struggling to release Alfie's hands too. 'You can touch it, Alfie. You should. That's it. Touch the bouncy castle!' And she stretched her own hands out to show him what she meant, hoping against hope that her theory would prove correct, and she wouldn't find herself dissolving instead of the creature.

Her fingers made contact with the slimy flesh of the worm; immediately they sank into the body, leaving a steaming trail shaped like two hands. 'It works! Do it, Alfie!' It was completely disgusting, sick-making even, but within a few moments the heat from four hands and, as far as she could bear it, two flushed Alfie faces, quickly reduced the enormous body to a pool of maroon slime.

At last they could see the door at the other end. 'Come on,' she yelled to Alfie, just as a blade glistened through the dragnet. She grabbed his arm with her sticky hand and pulled him through the viscous quagmire of melted ice-worm. Instantly she was reminded of being knee-deep in the bog at SPIcamp, so she unwound Alfie's SuSPInder, threw it so it connected with the door frame and activated the winding mechanism. 'Hang on, Alfie.' He grabbed her around the waist, and they water-skied through worm gloop until they smashed against the door. One quick fingerprint scan, and they were out.

'Won't my dad be looking for me? I mean, you.' said Alfie, bewildered.

'I've got some things to tell you,' shouted Janey as they battled through the buffeting wind. 'You're a Spylet, Alfie. A SPI in training.'

'Yeah, right!'

Janey smiled. Alfie was still definitely himself, even if he didn't remember his Spylet past. 'It's true. That's why you've got this gear on. And your dad is . . . well, let's just say he's not very nice.'

'How do you know?'

'Because . . .' Janey wondered what to say to persuade Alfie to come with her and not turn round to find his father. Behind them, spies, robot seals, probably divers in Navy Seals too, were organizing themselves into ranks ready to seek and destroy. Janey and Alfie were making little headway in the roaring torrent of wind, stopping as they were to have chats about their secret spy lives, and the gap between them and the enemy was dangerously small. Janey pulled Alfie's arm and looked into his eyes. 'We've got to go on.'

'Go on where?' yelled Alfie. 'We're on an iceberg!'

He had a point. SPUD Nik had disappeared back to base; they had no choice but to throw themselves into the freezing water and hope they made it to safe land – or ice – before the bitter temperatures or the Navy Seals got to them. Janey was just wondering how to tell Alfie, when they reached the edge of the iceberg and a dark voice boomed in her ear.

'Stay still and turn around, or we shoot.'

It was the bearded spy, grinning menacingly into his whiskers. Janey and Alfie slowly turned back to face their enemies. There were many, many of them, robotic seals and snowsuited spies, and in the distance behind them a vast dark shape slipping into the water. Suddenly the Retro-spectre of Copernicus strode to the front of the battalion, straight through several of the spies, who shuddered visibly.

'Kill Blonde!' he roared, pointing towards them.

Janey squinted so she couldn't see the bullet coming, then opened her eyes again when nothing happened. The bearded spy was staring uncertainly at Copernicus, at Alfie, and then back to her. 'Which one, sir?' he said eventually.

'The one who isn't my son, imbecile!' Copernicus flew across the ice towards them, then stopped. His eyes bored into hers, and Janey did her best to look as docile and dull as Alfie was as the moment. He switched his gaze to Alfie, who smiled blearily, despite the cold eating at his face. 'It's . . . it's . . . I don't know!' Copernicus stomped back to his cohorts. 'Capture them both,' he spat. 'We'll find out which it is under torture. It won't take long before the little girl folds like a house of cards.'

'He's really not nice, is he?' said Alfie, watching his father retreat.

The bearded spy stepped forward with another man, between them holding out the dragnet that Janey had stuffed into the hole. They were about to be captured like fish. Which gave Janey an idea.

'Alfie, you have this thing strapped to your leg. It's called an ISPIC.'

Alfie stared down at his thigh, bewildered. 'An ice pick? Where?'

'No, ISPIC. Oh, never mind. That board there will get us across the ocean,' she muttered out of the corner of her mouth. 'When I give the word, take it off, jump on it and head out across the water.'

'You're kidding, right?'

'Not if you don't want to die,' said Janey bluntly.

Alfie considered this for a moment, then nodded. The spies were nearly upon them, so Janey hissed,

'Something else: they'll catch us straight away with their Navy Seals unless we do something. You've got a chewy sweet in that pocket.' She pointed 'The minute you're on your ISPIC, chew it for one second, then throw it behind you.'

The net was outstretched to gather them up, the guns trained on their heads. 'NOW!' she bellowed.

In perfect unison they pulled the ISPICs from their thighs, pushed them over the edge of the ice towards the water and jumped on to the hovering boards. Alfie took a moment to steady himself, then turned to grin at Janey with such a look of deep joy that she laughed.

'Ha!' yelled Alfie. 'Weird, but . . . fun!' .

Janey showed him her own SPI-buy fruity chew. 'Right, chew, now!'

Already several metres out across the water, they were being followed by dozens of Navy Seals, who would be able to come up beneath them in moments. With perfectly synchronized timing, the pair of Alfies chewed their SPInamite wads once, twice, three times and then lobbed them over their shoulders into the water.

'Get ready to surf!' screamed Janey above the wind and the sound of mini-subs churning up the water behind them.

There was a minuscule delay, and then with a sudden sucking sensation the SPInamite detonated deep in the ocean. Navy Seals flew out of the water like real seals jumping for fish, and the first line of spies on the shore was blown off their feet and sent slithering across the ice. Janey looked back, motioning to Alfie to do the same, and then squatted low on her ISPIC.

The Southern Ocean surrounding Antarctica had never seen such a wave. Clinging on gamely to their ISPICS, and thanking SPI a million times over for the gravitational pull of the Fleet-feet, which made it almost impossible to come off them, Janey and Alfie slid up the slope as it rose ten . . . twenty . . . thirty metres into the sky. 'It's OK! I've done this before!' bellowed Janey as Alfie started to panic. She called just in time; at that instant the wave peaked, hovered as if frozen for a fraction of a second, then crested and broke. One minute the Spylet pair were hanging in mid-air over a jet-black mountain of water, the next they were flying along on a white-foam express train, swaying left and right over the bubbling crest of the wave, surfing like Hawaiians in the pitch dark, on a crashing crescendo of water that shot them across the sea as if they'd been fired from a cannon.

'This is the wickedest thing I've ever done!' hollered Alfie. 'Not that I can really remember what I've done . . . ooops,' as he traversed the slope to avoid a catastrophe, 'but I bet it is!'

And Janey laughed once, then again with surprise as Alfie's deep voice boomed out of her chest. 'I bet it is too!'

In mere moments they were cruising to a standstill, almost at the edge of the plate of ice housing Abe's Spylab. With their ISPICs hovering obediently a couple of inches above the water, they slid across to dry land and skidded to a halt in perfectly timed sweeping J-turns.

'Definitely wicked,' said Alfie, watching Janey and then strapping his ISPIC back to his leg.

There was just a hint of the old Spylet Alfie shining through his de-spied personality. Janey knew what they had to do to get the whole of it back again – put him through the DeSpies-U machine that removed all traces of spydom. Using it on the de-spied Alfie would reverse the process. 'Come on.' She pointed to the open doorway beyond the baying seals and penguins, who were in so much uproar they were almost stampeding.

Together they Fleet-footed along the corridors, with Alfie saying, 'Cool!' and 'This is really fast!' every so often, until they reached the Spylab. There was nobody there, so Janey ran around the room, looking for something that might be a DeSpies-U. 'Mirror,' she muttered. 'I'm looking for a mirror.' Eventually she discovered it. 'Of course!' It was the ice-plasma screen. With no images on it she could clearly see her reflection, and there was a conveniently placed chair just nearby. 'Alfie, come and sit over here.'

But just as Alfie walked over, shrugging his shoulders but doing whatever his strange double commanded, someone appeared in the doorway.

'Blonde, stop that right now.' Rook held out his Boy-battler, rocket-launcher finger poised ready to fire. 'I know it's you. I watched you Crystal-Clarify.'

So that was it. Copernicus had actually formed himself into Rook, had infiltrated the very heart of Solomon's Polificational Investigations, stolen Alfie away, and had now worked out which of the Alfies before him was his son and which was Jane Blonde, his nemesis. It explained the black marks, the assassinations, everything.

Janey stared right back at him. 'How could you do this to your own son?' she said bitterly.

Rook's face screwed up. 'What? I'm a kid, you idiot. How could *you* do this to your best mate? And betray your own father into the bargain?'

'What?' said Janey, confused.

'Yeah, I know what you're up to,' said Rook, his cocky strut bringing him closer to her so she could see the inky blackness of his SPIsuit clearly. 'You're about to de-spy Al Halo, you evil . . . What's the matter, can't you take the competition? Can't stand anyone else being as good a Spylet as you? This is all because Daddy didn't choose you at SPIcamp, isn't it?'

What was he talking about? Janey ploughed on. 'What have you done with my dad?'

Rook shook his head, looking at her as though she was mad. 'Nothing. I was just coming back to find him when I saw what you were about to do to Halo.

De-spying him so he forgets everything in his spying past, that's just plain mean. I can't let you do that. I'm going to make sure your dad knows, and then you'll be de-spied yourself.'

And suddenly Janey realized the truth – Rook was completely genuine. He thought she'd got the Spylet Al Halo and was about to de-spy him. He was *protecting* Alfie, not harming him. She couldn't explain the SPIsuit marks all over the place – unless it was Blackbird – but Rook was actually trying to help.

'Rook,' she said urgently, 'that's really you, isn't it? Look, we have to be quick. Alfie's already been de-spied by Copernicus, who I thought you were. We have to get the Spylet Alfie back. Prove it, Alfie.'

At that Alfie spun around in his chair. 'Hello, me. Hello, weird bird boy. Are we going to a fancy-dress party?' he said to Janey.

Rook's jaw sagged at the same time as his pointing middle finger. 'Jeepers, you'd better get on with it.'

So Janey pushed Alfie back in the chair, rolled it closer to the screen and said, 'Just relax and listen.' As soon as she heard the dark whisper of 'Halo, De-Spies-U' she backed away. There was no way she wanted to be de-spied herself, although, she thought suddenly, it would be nice to be Blonde again, not Halo.

'Rook, if you watched the Crystal Clarification,' she said quickly, 'do you think you could reverse it?'

'Piece of cake,' said Rook.

He certainly did seem to know what he was doing,
Janey decided, as her eyes began to droop and the 3-D
laser cast of Jane Blonde spinning above her got closer
and closer and closer. Minutes later, she was awoken
by an urgent tapping at the door.

'Alfie!' She leaped off the table and ran outside.

'Blonde, what are you doing hanging about in
there?' demanded Alfie. 'There are baddies to beat and
evils to eliminate.'

Janey grinned. 'Thanks, Rook,' she said. 'Seems
like we're all back to normal.'

But even as the words were leaving her lips, there
was a blood-curdling, gurgling scream from one of the
outlying rooms. All three Spylets took to their heels and
followed the noise.

'Oh no,' whispered Janey.

It was one of the scientists, slumped in the angle
of the corridor wall. Just near his hand was a small
revolver, as if he'd been trying to protect himself, but
had failed. His sightless eyes stared across the corridor,
his chin a mess of blood.

Janey felt sick to the core, and when she looked
around, both Rook and Alfie had turned as white as the
ice-walls of the corridor.

'Crushed. That only just happened,' said Alfie.
'Careful, everyone.'

Rook cocked his ear towards the door. 'Sounds
like more trouble. Listen to those animals.'

He was right. The two brave seals who had stayed behind at the SPI Spylab were barking and howling like marine werewolves, while the penguins were screeching and hooting as if their lives depended on it. Or someone else's. In the midst of it all was a terrific yowling that cut straight to Janey's heart.

Without a moment's thought, she sprinted for the exterior enclosure, Rook and Alfie close on her heels. The animals were going completely berserk, throwing themselves at each other, leaping into the sea and being tossed back out again by whatever stirred in the depths. Trouble was the worst of all, pelting headlong into the water, slashing madly with his sabre claw, and getting nowhere as some invisible force hurled him back, again and again, on to the pack ice.

'Trouble!' screamed Janey, running to gather him up, but then stopping short, frozen, completely unable to move when she saw what he had been trying to do.

'Oh my life,' said Alfie, screeching up behind her. 'Sick . . . squid,' he said faintly.

Rook chased after them as Janey and Alfie ran for the shoreline, but it was too late to do anything as the long legs of Abraham Rownigan disappeared under the water, dragged under by a gigantic monstrous tentacle. An evil yellow eye the size of a dustbin lid glinted balefully at them before the two sank below the surface.

'Oh! A colossal squid!' yelled Rook.

'It's a colossal monster,' said Alfie. 'Come on.'

And Janey knew the truth at last as she ran helplessly to the water's edge. The black marks had been squid ink, spilled out by the monster she had created when she had Satispied an evil overlord with a thousand other bodies – a giant squid. A colossal squid, as Rook had pointed out. It had been at Sol's Lols. It lived in a tank in the Spylab. It – he – had killed several innocent scientists by clamping a vast muscular tentacle around their chests and squeezing until their organs burst.

And now it had the one person she had vowed to save.

Alfie's dad, Copernicus the squid monster, was drowning her father.

sick squid

'I'm going after him!' Alfie sprinted for the edge of the pack ice. Whether it was Abe or his own father he was going after wasn't clear, but at least his shouting roused Janey from her nightmare state, rooted to the spot and incapable of action.

'You can't – you'll freeze to death,' she yelled after him. 'This way!'

Her heart almost in her throat, she ran, sobbing, towards the frenzied penguins. Only one of them was still, apart from the others, staring calmly out across the water, so Janey went straight to him, wrenched his head open and keyed in 'Abe' as quickly as her numbed fingers would allow her. Then she pushed the penguin over and shoved him like a toboggan so he slid gracefully along the ice and off the edge. 'Follow him, SPUD Nik! Send the messages back to my SPIV!'

Rook ran up behind her. 'Abe has Navy Seals

behind the penguins. Do you know how we can use them, Blonde?'

Without waiting to answer, Janey immediately sprinted for them. It *was* just like a nightmare; her legs felt like they were made of sponge, she seemed to be getting nowhere . . . and all the time her father was being pulled into the depths of the ocean by that monster, or having the last gasp of air squeezed out of him by a vicious gargantuan tentacle. 'Oh, Dad,' she stammered, sliding on the ice but righting herself just as the three spylets arrived at the robotic-looking seals lying dormant beyond the penguins.

'Like this!' Janey wrenched the tail to the left and the stopper clattered out on to the ice. She threw herself headlong into the Navy Seal, screaming, 'Close me in and push me into the water!'

Alfie tightened the stopper again and she felt the mini-sub slither into the icy depths. To her left, Rook was doing the same, and it looked as though Alfie would get left behind, until one of the scientists stumbled across to them and launched her friend into the water.

In formation, the three tiny submarines sped through the impenetrable darkness, the Spylet pilots unable to see more than a few centimetres beyond their seal's nose even with their Ultra-gogs. It was possible to work out where the others were only from the radar beeps being emitted at intervals and the two tiny red dots on the GPS screen in front of her.

Leaning over on to her side and still steering with her Gauntleted hand, Janey dragged her SPIV out from her Snowsuit and lay it next to the GPS. If SPUD Nik had any information, she needed to see it instantly.

What she saw first, however, was an insidious red shadow seeping across the edge of the GPS. 'There he is,' she spat. She was certain the shadow was the weaving Medusa-like body of Copernicus the Colossal Squid. Trying desperately to remember one of the many things they had learned at Spycamp, she twisted the knob marked 'Frequency' to number sixteen. 'Halo, Rook, can you hear me? There's a big shape ahead of us – I think it's them.'

'Rook here,' cracked a thin voice. 'Looks like you're right, and it's getting closer. I'll just . . . aaaargh!'

From the radio there came a deafening thump, and the GPS suddenly showed Rook's mini-sub being side-swiped; it rocketed across the display and disappeared off the edge of the screen.

'Rook! Rook, are you OK?' Janey peered frantically at the GPS, and spotted something else. 'Alfie, look out – you're about to be hit!'

'Righto.' Alfie sounded very calm about being thwacked by a sea monster that was actually his father. 'Left a bit, left a bit . . . I can see it . . . and . . . DROP! Ha. Missed me.'

'And I'm back too,' called Rook. 'Blonde, look out behind you.'

Instinctively Janey tried to turn round, but she was trapped inside the Navy Seal in a very fixed position, a sardine in a one-sardine can. She scanned the GPS. Just as Rook had warned, a long shadow like a giant's arm was sweeping towards her. It was too close; she had no time to avoid it, and any second now she would find herself rocketing sideways through the water as Rook had done.

But there was no great swipe from the tentacle. Janey looked at the GPS. The shadow was all around her. What was happening? Was Copernicus just toying with her? She braced herself for the blow, checking the GPS in confusion, but then she saw the shadow around her closing in and Janey realized, too late, what was going to happen.

'He's . . . crushing me!' she yelled, appalled, wriggling left and right as the sides of the min-sub buckled and bulged towards her, hemming her in, trapping her inside a mangled metal carcass that would surely split at any second. And then she'd be able to feel that slime-ridden, stinking tentacle smothering her face, squeezing the life out of her. 'No way,' she said, filled with revulsion for the monstrous man, and with something a lot more powerful.

Anger.

Just before her hand became completely trapped, Janey grabbed her SPIV and in the same movement spread Zinc or Zwim cream around the front of the mini-sub. It wasn't strong enough to melt through completely, but it weakened the structure so that Janey was then able to slice through the metal with her titanium blade. As she hacked her way out of her prison she felt the blade make contact with flesh, and the tentacle recoiled, only for a second or two, but just long enough for Janey to brace her hand against the little windscreen at the front of the Navy Seal, chewing her SPIder furiously as she activated her Fleet-Feet jump against the tail-end of the submarine. She rocketed out of the front of the Seal like a missile, a trail of bubbles splitting a cloud of squid ink in her wake. They were very deep in the water, far too deep for Janey to survive for long in the Antarctic temperatures, even in her extreme SPIsuit. She had simply swapped one unpleasant death for another, and she spun around helplessly as an enormous entity rushed by her.

Something brushed against her leg and she batted it away, convinced that it was a Copernicus tentacle. There it was again. She whipped around. And again! Only this time it was a definite nudge right behind her knees from something firm and snubby, not at all like the sharp point of a tentacle. Willing herself to stay calm, Janey trod water and tried to peer into the blackness. Suddenly a yellow eye loomed up in her face, and she screamed, only just stopping in time to prevent the SPIder from dropping out of her mouth. Another eye swivelled at her; to Janey's amazement, the two eyes were both smaller than her own, while the eye of the squid had been bigger than a dinner plate, and suddenly she understood. This was someone – something – trying to help her.

So she grabbed hold of the cylindrical body, lying full-length along the top of it, and allowed SPUD Nik to ferry her to the edge of the Copernicus camp iceberg. It took only moments with the SPUD powering through the ocean, so that Janey barely had time to register the intensity of the cold. The moment they hit the ice and saw the black shining trails leading across it, Janey hauled the penguin robot on to the ledge and then gave him an almighty push. A penguin would be able to pass by relatively unnoticed, while Jane Blonde most definitely would not. 'Go find Abe!' she hissed, and the SPUD scooted along on his belly, out of sight.

There was a gurgling noise from behind her; Janey dropped to the floor. Two Navy Seals popped up side by side, and Janey dared to lift her head to see if they were friend or foe. 'Penetrate!' she barked at her Ultra-gogs. To her relief Alfie's face, which would have been suffused with delight at finding such an amazing new form of transport were he not so worried about his friend, was peeking out from behind the one-way glass. She leaped to her feet and dragged both Seals from the water, opening the tail stoppers and extracting first Alfie and then Rook by the feet.

'Blonde! I thought you'd been squished,' said Rook, rubbing his cramped arms.

'It takes more than a bit of seafood to squish her,' said Alfie, trying to look cool, but thumping her on the arm to prove he was very glad to see her. 'Ah, I see my handsome old dad came this way.'

Janey's eyes smarted painfully. If Copernicus had passed by this way, then it was likely that her father had too, unless he'd been left at the bottom of the ocean. She didn't even know if he was still alive. Her chin quivered as she fought back tears, but she was distracted by a sudden beep from her SPIV.

'SPUD Nik! He must have seen something.'

Janey flicked through the images on the tiny screen: the grotesque caricature of Copernicus, three-quarters squid and only the tiniest part still human, sliding and lurching across the ice on his unearthly combination of limbs and tentacles; Copernicus looking back, his disgusting baggy squid head raw and open at the back of the neck and his eyes revoltingly mis-matched, with one huge circle of acid yellow and one bloodshot human eyeball; and then the one Janey most hoped to see – the end of one of Copernicus's tentacle-like arms (or were they arm-like tentacles? It was impossible to tell) looped around something long that was being pulled along the floor. Her father. As far as she could tell from the blurry image he was doing his best to uncoil the tentacle from around his waist. Janey's heart leaped. He was still alive!

And then her spirits plummeted once more as she scrolled through the next few photos that Nik had sent over. The first showed a phalanx of robot seals lined up around an icy precipice. On the next was a deep pink mass, hunching its way along behind them. An ice-worm. The third was the most disturbing, showing four enormously powerful cranes positioned around the edge of the precipice at which the seals sat, which Janey could now see was a gigantic hole in the ice. Each crane was pointed towards the centre of the hole, and suspended from their hooks was something Janey could not understand – it looked like a long metal tube, long enough to swallow a skyscraper, almost as tall as the rocket she had seen. And there, strapped helplessly to the bottom of it and looking barely bigger than an insect, was her father.

'He's at the tunnel,' she said, barely able to force the words out. 'The tunnel Copernicus has been digging towards the centre of the earth. He's going to drop him down it. Come on!'

The trio of Spylets forged forward, heaving seals out of the way, drop-kicking and Boy-battling any enemy spies that noticed them, and following at all times the bitter black trail left by Copernicus. The going was so strenuous that the blood started to pound in Janey's ears, and it almost felt as though it was getting darker. 'Floodlight!' she commanded her Ultra-gogs, and in seconds the miner's light had formed on her forehead so she could just about see the next few metres of Copernicus slime. The next moment, the harsh metal outline of a crane loomed into view, and Janey put her hand out to stop Rook and Alfie, whispering 'Floodlight off!' to her glasses. An element of surprise was what they needed now, and Janey gulped when she recalled that she had been taught that by G-Mamma as her very first rule of spying. 'Surprise, surprise, surprise,' she had said. Hopefully, whatever they did next would come as a nasty shock to Copernicus.

They crept forward, shielded by the darkness as they turned up their SPI-Pods to hear what was going on.

Copernicus's voice, bubbling and wet, was an atrocity, but what he actually said was even worse. 'It would have been fun to drown you, of course, but this has far more poetic justice. You will die at the exact moment I fulfill my dream.'

'Your dream is to destroy the planet? You're sicker than I ever imagined,' said Abe.

'Destroying the planet is just an unfortunate side effect.' Copernicus swivelled his enormous yellow eye towards his enemy. 'No, my plan is actually more along the lines of creation. And it was your darling daughter who helped me discover how to do it.'

Abe struggled against his bonds, shaking his head. 'Janey would never tell you anything, any more than your own son would if you didn't brain-wipe him.'

'Ah, but she did,' gurgled Copernicus in his foul, frothing voice. 'She told me exactly what's at the centre of the Earth, being the only human ever to have passed through it. We thought there'd be evidence at your headquarters, but no matter. It was all over her girly little drilling shoes anyway. A little bird brought them to me.'

Janey looked down at her SPILL-Drills, puzzled. The eSPIdrills? How had her shoes affected his plans? And how had he got hold of them? Just then a chilling noise boomed all around them.

'The cranes are starting up, Boz "Brilliance" Brown,' Copernicus cackled, his squid head snapping back and forth on the gnarled neck. 'I'm going to penetrate the centre of the Earth just at the moment you disintegrate into millions of atoms. Your tracer cells will be no use to you this time. Goodbye forever.'

Abe thrashed furiously, screaming, 'You'll kill your own son! The whole world! What's become of you?'

But Copernicus simply reached out with a tentacle and pushed a button on one of the cranes. A great rumbling arose, and then the cylinder started to descend into the bowels of the Earth.

Janey could barely see. Terror clouded her eyes. Blindly she stumbled forward, racing for

221

the edge of the tunnel, heading for her father. She'd saved him before, and she'd do it again. Only this time it sounded as though she'd be saving the rest of the world as well. Teardrops fell on her face and a roaring in her ears threatened to topple her off balance, but she drove on, forcing seals out of the way, burning sections of ice-worm to get through, and suddenly there was a clear path between her and the tunnel opening. With a good enough run-up she could leap on to the cylinder and shimmy down to her dad.

But as she sped up, the teardrops spattered more thickly against her face and the roaring in her ears rose in a crescendo – only they weren't tears, they were snowflakes, falling thick and fast, so thick it was like being suspended in milkshake. Chips of ice flew all around and the world started to spin around Janey, as if she was trapped inside a giant spinning tube, a tube of white walls, with no beginning and no end . . .

Janey staggered, falling to her knees, disorientated, unable to work out where she was going or to stop a tide of nausea from engulfing her. As her surroundings went black, Janey realized that her knees had not made contact with the ground. She was free-falling. Tumbling. Straight down the tunnel.

tunnel of terror

'Janeeeeeeeeey!'

Abe's anguished scream penetrated the dense black soup of her mind. Where was she? In a mineshaft – wasn't it something like that? That's what the red-haired girl had said. Something about a mineshaft. And where exactly had Titian Ambition disappeared to?

Janey opened her eyes to have a look, and it all came back to her, all at once, as she somersaulted through space. She was in the tunnel that Copernicus the Squid had created, and right behind her, being lowered towards the hard metal core of the Earth, was a giant cylinder with her father stuck on the outside of it like a bug. At the moment they were still bypassing ice and tight-packed snow, with occasional gushes of water where the pressure was starting to affect the sides of the structure, with the lake below the glacier spurting through the cracks. Pretty soon they would start to pass through warmer sections, the magma, and then eventually past the scrabbling volcanic shrimps.

At which point Janey and her father would dissolve in the centre of the Earth.

And in that moment she finally understood what Copernicus was doing. It *was* a mineshaft. He was mining. He was plucking out the metallic core of the Earth – or at least some of it – and stealing it, without any regard for the devastation it would cause to the whole of the rest of the world. It was what he'd been telling Alfie: the earth needed that metal for gravity. And who had told him it was there? Janey. Janey and her eSPIdrills had given him the exact information that he needed to destroy the planet – the planet that had refused to give him the power he wanted. It was her fault.

Janey tried to clear her head but the world, or rather the inside of it, was rushing by at such speed that she couldn't tell which way was up. She had to slow down, slow down her father and the awful metal tube that was going to grind him into the lava and then stamp a great cylinder through the iron core of the earth. She passed close to the wall and tried to reach out for a shrimp anchored to a platform, but she was dropping at such speed that the whole lot just came away in her hand and plunged down the tunnel ahead of her. Her father was close by too; Janey could see the terror in his face, and understood instantly that it was not terror for himself, or even for her, but for the disaster that was about to befall the whole planet. She had to slow down!

Something new was shooting down towards her, just in her field of vision. It was an enormous snowball. An avalanche? It was hurtling directly towards her, as if she wasn't already going fast enough! When this thing hit her she would be snookered straight down the tube to a hot and sticky end. Then she heard her father shout out, and looked up to see if she could avoid the snowball. It was big, as big as a volcanic shrimp, or possibly a . . . an Arctic tern? It was big enough and white enough – that had to be what it was. But then Janey saw four little black cloven hooves whizzing towards her. Hooves? It had to be a sheep! A flying sheep – Maddy, the wonderful sheep who had been used and abused by Copernicus for his cloning experiments, but who turned into a pellet-firing flying machine when she Wowed. And strapped underneath her was a gold-and-green-eyed Spycat, reaching out for her.

'Trouble! Maddy!' Janey wanted to cry, she was so pleased to see them before she died. They raced down towards her so that Trouble was dangling within arms' reach. She held out her hand to stroke his ridiculous quiff – and suddenly it came to her, her very last bit of spy training before she left SPIcamp. There was something she'd been about to do before the tube of terror had made her pass out. This time she was surviving the terror. She could cope.

'Now, Blonde!' she screamed, forcing herself into action. 'Dad, hold tight! Really tight! I'm coming.' She had no idea if her father could hear her as she reached for Trouble's collar and took hold of the tiny glass ball that was hanging there. Almost sobbing with relief, Janey felt the wind whistle against her palm, then force itself out between her fingers before blasting out against the walls of the tunnel, upwards against the descending tube with her father on it, and down into the depths of the earth, splattering volcanic shrimps against the sides and sending any that weren't hanging on flying off into the lava. The vortex was fully operational. Above her head was a noise like a rocket, and she looked up, expecting to see Copernicus escaping, but instead watching the metal tube – and her dad – catapult back up the tunnel at hundreds of miles an hour. It was about to shoot out of the top like a cork from a champagne bottle, shattering the four cranes and leaving Copernicus's mission in tatters.

Of course, it might just leave her father in tatters too. Janey hugged Maddy and Trouble to her tightly, cushioned inside the vortex and wedged tightly inside the tunnel.

'We'd better get out of here.'

Janey looked around. They were hovering on

compressed air. The centre of the Earth was just a speck many thousands of metres below them, but they were very close to the tube she had created with her SPILL-Drills. 'This way,' she called, and she walked backwards on air, tugging Maddy with one hand while keeping a tight hold of Trouble's glass ball with the other. They struggled through the clamouring, rushing wind at the edges of the Spyroscope's fixed vortex, Janey pushing Maddy ahead of her up the tube she'd made. The pressure of the wind inside the tiny tunnel turned them into champagne corks too, and the three of them raced up the tube, hanging on to each other grimly as they slid ever upwards and then burst out of the top to spill, panting, out on to the ice.

'You saved us!' Janey hugged Maddy and buried her face in Trouble's extra-luxuriant fur. 'Oh, you clever animals, you saved us!'

'Hey, you Abe's babes! Good job they thought of it all on their own, isn't it?' said a voice over her head.

Janey threw her arms around her SPI:KE's ankles. 'G-Mamma! You're here too. I'm so glad to see you.'

'And us, I hope,' drawled another familiar voice.

She looked up to find a host of familiar faces looking down at her – Alfie, Mrs Halliday, Leaf, Rook and, of course, Bert (now known as the Australian spy Dubbo Seven, according to the label on his khaki SPIsuit). 'You're all here.' It was slightly embarrassing as she was sprawled on the floor, wrapped around

G-Mamma and a couple of spy-pets.

'We have all been in training,' said Leaf. 'Heard you might be in a bit of a mess down here.'

Janey's relief and joy evaporated instantly. 'And Dad still is. He got shot out of the tunnel attached to that tube thing. He could have been fired anywhere.'

'Incoming,' barked G-Mamma.

They all whipped around as one. A strange and bedraggled group of spies and spy-creatures was lumbering towards them – an ice-worm, doing its best to avoid being touched by anything else, was leading the way, bringing with it a wedge-shaped army of Copernicus spies, enormous volcanic shrimps and a couple of dozen Navy Seals pointing straight at them, alarmingly like a row of cannons.

Janey shouted out everything she could remember. 'The worm just melts if you touch it with your bare skin – gross, but it works. The shrimps have sharp pincers but they can't see, and I don't think they like the cold. The spies are just, well, evil, and I'm most worried about the Navy Seals. They've got a "launch missile" button in them.'

As if to prove her point, at that very second the bearded spy yelled an instruction at his group and they all dropped to their knees, covering their heads.

'They are thinking they will blow us up,' yelled Leaf. 'Maddy, take me over there!'

Maddy rose into the air obediently, and Leaf

jumped for her legs. He was so skinny that his weight had little effect on her ability to fly, and he steered her straight towards the missile that was about to open up. 'Cover me!' he shouted, and immediately G-Mamma jumped up and down, shouting, 'Come and get me!' as Alfie, Bert and Rook let loose with their heat-seaking missiles. Before the enemy group could work out what was happening, Leaf had scissored his legs around the missile from above, turned it around and sent it rocketing across the ice, taking half the other missiles with it. They plunged over the edge of the tunnel and could be heard a few seconds later, detonating harmlessly in the great abyss.

G-Mamma, meanwhile, headed straight for the worm, her pink SPIsuit matching the florid skin of the ice-creature almost perfectly. 'Think you can copy my look and get away with it? I don't think so.' She reached out her ring-bedecked hands to reduce it to soup, but the worm was already slithering away in the opposite direction. It might not be able to see, but a mad G-Mamma was still easy to sense.

'Shrimps for us, then,' yelled Janey, signalling to Mrs Halliday. She flung the end of her SuSPInder to the SPI:KE, who attached it to her own as she unravelled it across the ice. Between them they held a chain the length of a football pitch.

'Now!' yelled Janey, and in formation they Fleet-footed across the ice. As soon as they neared the mass of volcanic shrimps, Halo held firm as Janey raced on her ISPIC in a gigantic arc, right around them. 'Pull!' she shouted as she drew near to the SPI:KE, and as Mrs Halliday and Janey crossed each other, the SuSPInders formed a tightening circle around the creatures. They'd been lassoed together, and no amount of wiggling and scrabbling would get them out.

'Hey, bonza, ladies!' called Bert, stunning an attacking spy with his boomerang. 'I'll put you to work at Dubbo Seven.'

But just at that moment Janey's SPIV beeped, and a clear video image sprang up – her father's face, battered and bloody, but twitching as he dragged himself back across the ice cap, past the smouldering mess of gooey, contorted metal. His strained features stood out clearly; he had to be leaning on SPUD Nik who was busy taking panaromic views of his surroundings. Cranes, robotic seals, ice-worms, the metal cylinder – all lay mangled about the iceberg, inoperative or just plain dead. 'All the seals are dealt with,' said G-Mamma, looking around her at the thwarted, exhausted enemies. 'Come on then, spies and Spylets. Let's go help our noble master.'

The relief team of spies had come well prepared, with G-Mamma and Bert sharing a shimmering white skidoo, Maddy and Trouble co-piloting a low flight overhead, and all the Spylets on advanced ISPICs.

Janey ripped her own from her thigh and shot across the iceberg, swerving and ducking to avoid the twisted ironwork around the mouth of the tunnel. The gaping hole in the planet looked like an open artery, with lava, steaming water and occasional volcanic shrimps spewing from it from time to time. 'We really need to fill in that hole,' thought Janey.

As she knew the way better than anyone, she was well ahead of the group as they drew level with her father. Screeching to a halt, she clamped him tight around the middle. 'Dad! You're OK. You're OK!'

'Janey.' It was all her father could say as he sagged against her, kitten weak and bleeding from all manner of scratches and wounds.

But in the background Janey had spotted something – a dark, twisted shape, gnarled as an old tree, slithering in the opposite direction across the iceberg. 'He's heading for the black labyrinth!'

'Who?' Rook asked.

'Copernicus. He's going to get away again! Let's go after him. Oh', she said, turning back to her father, 'do you mind if I borrow SPUD Nik?'

'Be my guest,' said her dad, sinking to his knees as he let go of the penguin.

G-Mamma was already shimmying to a stop beside him, so Janey programmed the SPUD quickly and set off after him across the ice, with Alfie, Leaf and Rook in hot pursuit.

In no time they were at Copernicus's labyrinth. Janey didn't even pause to get off her ISPIC – just pressed her rocket-launcher finger ahead of her and blasted her way through the door, yelling 'Floodlight!' to her obedient Ultra-gogs. She X-rayed every wall, looking for the disgusting slithering mass of colossal squid. The ice-worm stables were empty, as were the recreation hall and bedrooms, but as Janey swished into the Spylab through the Zinc-creamed hole she'd made in the door earlier, she was confronted by something very unexpected.

It was Copernicus, the man. And standing uncertainly to his side was Alfie.

Janey jumped off her board. 'Alfie, what . . . ?'

Copernicus sneered at her. 'You are not, I repeat, not going to stop me, Blonde. Your imbecilic theatricals have cost me this leg of the mission only, but you've given me enough information, and I've got enough metallic ore, to do what I planned. And if you want your friend to survive, you'll turn around right now and leave.'

Alfie lifted his hands to Janey, his eyes confused. He barely appeared to recognize her. He looked young, vulnerable and less sarcastic than Janey had ever seen him, even when brain-wiped. She couldn't possibly let him be hurt.

'All right,' she said slowly. 'I'll go . . .'

He'll shoot me in the back, she thought as she

turned around slowly. Why wouldn't he shoot me in the back? Maybe Alfie wouldn't let him. Or . . . or maybe he can't! She paused for just a fraction of a second, then jumped back on her ISPIC and swished it around with her heel. 'Sorry, Alfie, if this really *is* you.'

And she pushed off, heading straight for them. Alfie's eyes widened slightly but Copernicus looked furious, right at the moment when she passed through the pair of them and out the other side. They were Retro-spectres, both of them – that was why Alfie had suddenly looked so young. His image had been taken from an old photo. The real Alfie was clattering around in the corridors outside, and all the time she was there, chatting with the ghostly Alfie, the real Copernicus was getting away.

Fortunately SPUD Nik had been well programmed and was bashing himself against the ice wall at the far side of the lab, just as Alfie, Rook and Leaf spun into the room. 'It's nothing,' she yelled over her shoulder.

'It's freaky,' said Alfie, looking at himself yet again. 'And what the heck's that noise?'

'No, it's really nothing – a couple of Retro-spectres. Come here, would you? We need your Boy-battlers.'

All three boy Spylets jumped instantly back on their ISPICs, joining Janey at the far wall. On her instruction they lined up their Boy-battlers and acid-sprayed the half-metre-thick ice separating the lab

233

from what lay beyond. Even before she could see it, Janey had a good idea what it was going to be.

She was right. It looked different from when she had first seen it: all the scientists and the circular platforms they'd been standing on had disappeared, and the rocket, quivering, was emitting spouts of gas and a huge amount of noise. Way above their heads, in what must have been the peak of the iceberg, the stars twinkled intermittently through the swirling snow – the whistling, tormenting snow that would never again get the better of Jane Blonde.

'Wow, will you look at that?' said Rook.

'It is not good, I think.' Leaf was looking the rocket up and down with expert eyes. 'We had better get out of the way. It will take off in about thirty seconds.'

'There!' screamed Janey, pointing at the small porthole near the base of the rocket. 'He's in there. He's got his bit of ore and that Supersizer thing, and he's going to get away and do something awful again. We have to stop him!'

Alfie pulled at her arm. 'There's nothing we can do about it!' His hair blew around in the rushing fumes from the rocket. 'You have to get back.'

'But he was going to destroy the planet! He'll try again!'

It was more than Janey could bear. The monster about to make his escape had almost killed them all. There had to be something they could do. But Rook was tugging at her other arm, while Leaf had started the countdown at twenty.

'I can't . . . I have to think of something!'

'Give it up, Janey,' roared Alfie.

But she couldn't. She pushed the others back through the door. 'I'm going to have to make a sacrifice. Go on! It's the only way.'

As Alfie shook his head, with Rook dragging him backwards and Leaf screaming out, 'Eight, seven, six . . .' Janey grabbed the equipment she needed and began her very own countdown.

spud nik in space

'Nik, even though I know you're just a robot,' she said, winking into the back of his throat and twisting the top of his head backwards, 'we will never, ever forget you. But I guess it's time to see whether penguins can fly.'

She programmed in the words 'Copernicus, volcanic shrimps', planted a large kiss on SPUD Nik's beak and lay down on the floor. Even as Leaf's disappearing voice yelled, 'Three . . . Two . . . you had better be coming now, Blonde. One!' she heard Nik poddle towards the rocket.

The room, in fact the whole of the iceberg, shook like a daisy in a gale as the rocket ignited, lifted a few feet off the floor and then hovered for blast-off. Janey dared to glance upwards, protected from the searing heat by her SPIsuit and Ultra-gogs, and there was the noxious, squelching head of Copernicus, pressed against the porthole. Even from this distance she could see that he was laughing, triumphant, convinced that he had escaped to whatever distant planet he was heading for.

Little did he know that SPUD Nik, barely even blistering in the heat, was intent on a search and photograph mission. As the control tower room exploded around Janey and the rocket launched up through the open panel towards the stars, a small black and white shape followed it, anchoring itself in the workings of the rocket as the SPUD tried to reach Copernicus to take photos. SPUD Nik entered the fuselage and inched his way upwards, ever upwards, trying to reach Copernicus to get a photograph. It blinked on to Janey's SPIV, a clear picture of the vile, destructive demon squid. Nik rattled a few more photographs across, and then he did what Janey knew he would. He followed his next order.

'You go, SPUD Nik,' she whispered.

They were several miles up in the air, and Janey could swear that she could hear the distant crowing of a squid who thought he'd won the battle, when the rocket suddenly faltered and shook, and the engine burners closed down. One peck of a beak had been all that was needed for the penguin to fulfil his mission. The next minute, the whole rocket was dropping out of the sky, heading straight for the volcanic shrimps that SPUD Nik had been programmed to find and photograph. On her SPIV, Janey could see the Earth rushing towards her, and it took her a moment to realize that she was seeing exactly what the penguin was recording. In nano-seconds the warped engineering at the top of the tunnel came into view, and then the rocket was crashing down the tunnel, ravaging the walls, plunging through water and ice and lava as the great horrible tube collapsed in on itself, filling in, disappearing, plugged by a rocket the size of a skyscraper, completely entrapping Copernicus.

Janey struggled to her feet as the images from the SPIV grew dimmer and finally disappeared. 'Thank you, SPUD Nik,' she said sadly. He might not have been a real animal, but he'd certainly been a very real friend.

The ground around her was shaking, separating, plates of ice being ripped apart and floating off across the labyrinth. The Spylab walls were disintegrating, and Janey knew that she had only moments to get out of there. Jumping from one ice platelet to another, she navigated her way across to the Spylab door, and then ISPIC'd as she had never done before, dodging falling ice-plasma screens and Retro-spectre machinery, swerving around the wall of the ice-worm stables that bulged outwards before cracking apart under the pressure, and crouching close to the ground to race out through the exterior door before it collapsed completely.

She sped to where she had left her father, watching the amazed expressions of her colleagues and friends as she hurtled towards them. 'Get out of here!' she yelled. 'The whole iceberg's going to disappear down the tunnel!' She shot past Alfie, who looked suspiciously as though he might have been about to cry, and led the way back across the ice, racing against time and subverted nature as the iceberg creaked and sagged and finally, with a great groaning scream like a huge animal dying, imploded into the tunnel, closing over the top completely so that it might never have existed.

They all turned to look from the safety of the penguin enclosure at Abe's Spylab. The king penguins were relatively calm now; one or two of the seals had even rejoined their group, and even though they were all still twitchy, the panic of the previous few days had disappeared.

'Your dad was in there,' she said to Alfie.

For a moment she thought he was a little upset. The creature might be a monster, but he was still his father, after all. But then Alfie rounded on her. 'You idiot! You said you were making a sacrifice, and I thought . . . we all thought . . . I think . . . you're an idiot!'

'Oh, thanks for saving all our lives, Blonde. Thanks for getting rid of Vicious Squid once and for all. Thanks for stopping the planet from exploding, Blonde.' G-Mamma stood protectively behind Janey. 'But we understand, don't we, girly-girl? It's difficult seeing your friends and loved ones do something dangerous, maybe even life-threatening.'

Alfie turned scarlet. 'She's not a l . . . a what you said. A friend, kind of, maybe, but . . .'

'Oh, shut up, Alfie,' said Mrs Halliday pleasantly.

Janey was looking at her dad. He was nodding, agreeing with what G-Mamma had just said, and as she saw his expression something finally became clear. 'Dad,' she said softly, 'you know when you didn't choose me for the team – *was* it because I kept flaking out in that terror-tube thing?'

He shook his head as he held out his arms. 'No, Janey. It's because you're my daughter. Way up on the assassination list, and most likely to try to sacrifice yourself for me. I just couldn't bear to lose you.'

They walked into the white labyrinth together. Just a normal spy family, thought Janey with a sigh.

Despite the pain from his injuries, Abe wasted no time in gathering everyone together for a debrief. A bunch of worried-looking scientists grouped themselves around the outsides of the Spylab, while the SPIs clustered in the middle.

'It's over, for now.' Abe rubbed his hand across his eyes. 'The mystery of the animals has been cleared up – the electromagnetic field had been completely disrupted by Copernicus tunnelling through the planet. He was about to carve out a chunk of the Earth's core and cart it away in his rocket, which, by the way, would have caused the whole planet to tip and be destroyed. Instead, thanks to a rather sensational Spylet and her friends, said rocket has filled up the tunnel and order is restored.'

A few of the scientists let out half-hearted cheers, and there was a ripple of applause from the outer edges of the room. Abe held up his hand. 'It's not really a time to celebrate. We've believed before that Copernicus has been thwarted, and he's come back to haunt us again. Literally, this time, as a Retro-spectre. The threat is ever present. Let's stay alert.'

Janey looked around at the sombre collection of spies. It was the first occasion she'd had time to work out that not everyone was there. 'Blackbird,' she whispered.

Rook looked down at his feet.

'Oh no. She was the "little bird" who gave Copernicus my eSPIdrills.'

'I sent her to doctor those cards your mum had painted,' said Abe. 'So that you'd feel . . . you know.' Like spying again, guessed Janey. 'It seems she took the opportunity to betray us at the same time.'

'No!' Rook's sharp little face glared from one to the other of them. 'She wouldn't do that! I reckon she was jealous of Blonde and just wanted to try out those shoe things.'

'Well, we'll only know for sure when she tells us herself,' said Abe.

Janey sighed. Spying had seemed like a bit of a game when she'd started. Now it was getting incredibly serious, right down to saving the

241

whole Earth from destruction. Suddenly she wanted a bit of normality and a hug from her mum.

'Oh no!' she exclaimed. 'Mum!'

Going a little pink as the SPIs around her laughed, Janey tried to calculate how long she'd been away from home. 'I was meant to just go to bed, but I must have been here ages! She'll have called the police and everything.'

'No, she hasn't,' said a familiar voice from the doorway.

Janey turned around, and in walked . . . herself. She gulped. Her cloned twin was back! 'Chloe?'

Even Rook laughed, despite his flushed face. 'Just hang on a minute,' he said.

He disappeared into the CC room with the other Blonde. A few minutes later he emerged, accompanied by a red-headed girl with a gap-toothed grin.

'Tish!' Janey stared. 'You were me?'

Tish shrugged. 'Rook and I saw you Crystal-Clarify, and I thought that was a pretty brave thing to do. Like I said: sometimes, Blonde, I like your style. So I decided the most helpful thing I could do was pretend to be you so your mother didn't start upsetting the apple cart back at home. Rook CC'd me and I've been standing in for you there, and eating some totally disgusting food.'

Janey couldn't help herself. 'Did she do that speed-dating thing?'

'I'm obviously not half as nice as you.' Tish smiled broadly. 'After a few of my "smart comments", they ran away faster than a Spylet on an ISPIC.'

'Wow. Thanks,' said Janey.

'Actually, your mum was pretty pleased. I don't think she was really that keen. Seems to have fond memories of someone else.' And Tish grinned cheekily at Abe.

Janey could hardly understand it. She had been so determined not to trust anyone, especially Rook and Titian Ambition, but it had just dawned on her that the only thing wrong with Tish was that she always said exactly what was on her mind, for good or ill, and maybe that wasn't so bad, after all. And what they'd done between them had been really special. 'We're . . . we're a really good team.'

'And I've been promoted, Zany Janey!' G-Mamma pointed to the large diamanté brooch on her lapel. 'Look – SPI:NE – SPI: Newbie Educator. I can train SPIs as well as Spylets now.'

'You were . . . just training Bert?' said Janey.

'Well, what else would I be zipping off to Oz for the whole time?' G-Mamma rolled her eyes and helped herself to a doughnut.

Janey shook her head as theSPIs and scientists dispersed, some fussing over Maddy and Trouble as if they were their own pets and others desperate for a clean-up and a lie-down. Lingering behind, she waited for a moment alone with her father.

'I have to go home, Dad,' she said. 'Are you coming too?'

'Yes.' Abe wrapped his battered arms around her. 'I just can't say when.'

'As long as you don't say "never",' said Janey.

Because that was the truth of it. As long as there was hope, she could always be exactly what she was today – half schoolgirl Janey Brown and half spylet Jane Blonde. Brown and Blonde. Blonde and Brown. It was getting harder and harder these days to tell the difference.

abe's babes

Janey smiled at her father as she prepared to Satispy. Given what the planet had just been through, it seemed a better option than SPILL-Drilling though the Earth. Tish and Rook had already left on a tiny plane piloted by Leaf and Ivan, and Alfie and his mother were going to Navy Seal as far as they could before Satispying back from southern Europe. Janey thought it was an awfully long time to be trapped in a tin, but they'd both seemed pretty excited about it. And they'd be safe – Trouble and Maddy were keeping an eye on them from the air.

Jane Blonde waved briefly. 'Bye, Dad. Keep in touch.'

Abe Rownigan smiled as he held out the remote control.

'Hey, skiddaddle, Pengy-poo!' G-Mamma flurried into the Spylab, flapping her hands at something in the corridor behind her. 'Out with your other weirdy brothers.'

But Janey recognized the lumbering walk as the ragged penguin waddled towards her just as her cells began to separate.

SPUD Nik! She called out his name but her voice had evaporated to nothingness. He'd come back to complete his mission, like every good spy should.

And Janey's disintegrating lips curved into a smile. She'd be back too, to finish whatever mission she was needed for next. Whenever that might be, the Sensational Spylet would be ready.